SEDUCED BY THE OUTLAW

Apollonia Lord

CRIMSON ROMANCE™

F+W Media, Inc.

Published by
Crimson Romance™
an imprint of F+W Media, Inc.
10151 Carver Road, Suite 200
Blue Ash, OH 45242, U.S.A.
www.crimsonromance.com

ISBN 10: 1-5072-0132-X
ISBN 13: 978-1-5072-0132-9
eISBN 10: 1-5072-0133-8
eISBN 13: 978-1-5072-0133-6

CHAPTER ONE

1896
Kansas City, Missouri

"I have come to place a lonely hearts ad."

Tamar Freeman jumped at the booming voice that cut through the silence of the *Advocate*'s office. A lady journalist such as herself shouldn't jump out of her composure and skin at the slightest sound. *But I am not an ordinary journalist*, she thought, attempting to reign in her nerves and exhaustion. *The Advocate* was the only newspaper in the area for the colored citizens—black, brown, and tan-hued men and women—who made Kansas City their home. She didn't write about home and hearth, recipes and religion. She was a crusader for truth and justice. As the lone colored woman publishing a newspaper in the state, she made some friends and many angry enemies who were upset with her editorials. Threats were commonplace. She just hoped that this week she could live in peace.

The bronze colored gentleman cleared his throat and primed the bell on the counter. The chime echoed through the office. She glanced around at the storefront's three cramped rooms and grimaced. It could hardly be called an office with all the things she had crammed in here.

Again, he spoke. "Ma'am, I have come to place a lonely hearts ad," he said, clutching his hat in a death grip. His eyes looked over every bit of the room as if he was making sure no one could surprise him from any angle.

Tamar's youngest sister Delilah placed the form on the counter. "Sir, complete this. Have you written one before?"

The man harrumphed, his loud exhale rumbled through the space and possibly the barbershop next door. "Too many to count. Love is a vain and cruel mistress."

Delilah clucked like a mother hen, her soft face beaming with joy and happiness. "But you cannot give up hope. Love is superb and worth it."

"My dear, you are young and naïve. Heartbreak has a way of grinding you down to where the hurt and pain isn't worth it. It's never worth it."

"Delilah!" Tamar called her to the back of the room. "Take care of these for me," she said, handing the scissors and twine to her sister. Tamar had learned the lessons of love the difficult way and at forty knew what the man was talking about. Delilah was twenty years younger than she was and was filled with fanciful hope and cheer. No old codger was going to convince her that love and adventure were impossible to have without trouble and melancholy. "These have to get ready for distribution before we run the next edition." The paper had moved to a twice a week publication schedule. A big reason for the success of the paper was the lonely hearts ads. The hard and lonely life on the farms and towns drove people to sell love any way they could. Luckily, they came to the *Advocate* to find love, and wrote to the Agony Aunt column to keep it. Her sister's suggestions for fun and diversions in the newspaper had made her a tidy profit but she hoped that people read the news and politics pieces too. She had a sinking suspicion that no one cared about progress and civil rights as much as she did.

The amount of work and manpower needed to make the operation grow was staggering. She could afford the help, but did she need the headache? For ten years, she'd struggled to make this paper a success, borrowing and scraping what she could to make her dream a reality. Now they had it—but with a steep price.

As if in answer to her thoughts, a rock crashed through the plate glass window. The man jumped in surprise, but the two Freeman women continued to work. The man started for the door, his hand on the doorknob and his feet ready to chase before Tamar stuck two fingers in her mouth, and whistled. "Sir, I'd advise you to not pursue."

"Someone demolished your property."

"The someone is the Klan," Delilah piped up from the back.

Tamar sighed. Her sister gave little thought about discretion and believed all of the skin folk were fans of the radical leaning paper. "It's not the Klan," she said loud enough for her sister to hear. It was a lie. She was certain of it, but it was easier to keep her sister's mind free of worry and anxiety.

"May I?" Without waiting on her answers, the man snapped a dazzling white handkerchief from his coat's pocket and scooped up the rock. "What do we have here?" He peeled the white paper wrapping off the rock and stretched it taut on the counter. His face blanched as much as a man the color of mud could. "Inappropriate and vile. No lady should read this."

"I'm no lady." She pulled the post close to her for inspection. The words formed mean and ugly statements about her and explicitly stated that her office would burn, before going into how much better her slim neck would look with a noose around it. Clearly she had made some people angry with her last few statements about the segregation of schools and the rampant lynchings happening across the country. These were things one was supposed to accept as a part and parcel of life. She wasn't going to accept anything but full human rights and dignity. Good—that's what she was supposed to do. Put clamps on those who made the lives of others impossible to live, even if she had to suffer intimidation and terror. "This is tame in comparison," she muttered.

"In comparison to what?"

Tamar shook her head at the gentleman. This was no time to discuss the awful nature of mankind as evidenced by her piles of hatred mail. The letters arrived and she shoved them into drawers without opening them. A woman could only take so much disparagement and hate in a day. "It is not important. The men and women who write this hateful trash will not stop me from my work, so how may I help you today?" she asked, twisting a smile and pleasant look onto her face.

The man's concerned face didn't budge. "You should call for the sheriff."

"Ha," she said, stuffing the offensive notice into a drawer. "I have darkened his door several times. He said I can't prove anything."

"They wrote their name on it," the man said with a grumble. "That's from the Ku Kluxers. I didn't realize they were prominent in this area."

"Well, they are. And the sheriff has an affinity for that group, being a former rebel. He's not a man we go to for security or assistance. Now, enough about that. May I see your lonely hearts request?" Tamar snatched the piece of paper from under the heel of his hand and squinted at the mash-up of hieroglyphics and chicken scratch all over the page. "I cannot read this." She passed it back to him.

He chuckled, folding the note into tight quarters and tucking it into his pocket. "My handwriting is abysmal. Let me dictate my words to you." He took a deep breath and started to compose his note. "Ada, my dear. You have gone astray. I am certain I have lost you. I will move on alone. This is your last chance; give me a sign. Meet me where we last met before you broke my heart."

She raised her hand to stop the stream of words from his mouth. "Just a warning—we charge by the word."

"Money's no object. I need to get that off my chest."

Whoever this woman was had surely hurt this man. Tamar was certain of that. Her normal prying questions danced on her tongue and she yoked them into submission. Asking questions to the brokenhearted led to long discussions, lamentations about the curses of love, and crying jags. *And I have time for none of that*, she thought. She had to go through the newspapers and insights she collected from the mail and set type. "Is that all you have to say to her? Most men want to end with a declaration of love or promise of intentions."

Delilah piped in. "Or at least tell her that you forgive her and all can be made well."

The crumbling of the hard look on his face confirmed Tamar's thoughts. A reconciliation was not going to happen. "I gave you all the words I had. I trusted her. She broke my trust. I waited and still no response."

"I'm so sorry," she said, patting his heavy hand. For a large man with fists that resembled mallets, his skin was soft. "She will come back to you. This Ada."

"I don't have high hopes. She ruined my plans."

"Strange," Delilah muttered, wandering back into the room. "A woman named Ada has been mentioned many times in the recent love matches pages."

Tamar swirled around and shot her sister a withering look that caused her to retreat and shush her mouth. It was true. Ada had been a popular woman. Messages had been flying back and forth between Ada and several suitors. That dexterity of balancing suitors and their interests and needs was more drama and work than any woman in her right mind needed. And Tamar was in her right mind. The man didn't need to know that his one-time love was collecting admirers across the plains. "It will be three dollars."

The man unfurled several bills from his money clip. "Make it as large as possible."

The size of type didn't show the strength of love, but Tamar would take the money and set the press for his desire.

"Am I done here?" the man asked.

"Of course. We will take care of this."

"And if you need anything related to that window … " The man dropped a calling card on the counter. "Let me know."

Tamar nodded, holding her grimace until the man left. She would take care of the window later with a dispatch to the handyman she used for times like this. She had lined his pockets more in the past few months than ever before. She glanced at the card, then read it again to make sure her eyes hadn't deceived her. Bart Quarles, primary investigator, Pinkerton national detective agency. Curiosity tickled her brain. Pinkertons were celebrated and notorious for their investigations and union busting. What was a Pinkerton agent doing here? And who exactly was Ada? Tamar checked the personal ad and dismissed the last question. Pinkerton agent or not, he was a man sustaining a broken heart. Those were common for any human.

CHAPTER TWO

Ada, my dear. You have gone astray. I am certain I have lost you. I will move on alone. This is your last chance; give me a sign. Meet me where we last met before you broke my heart.

The man known as Deadwood Dick in the company of robbers lazily perusing the newspaper, lollygagging in the manner customarily pinned to him. The men here thought that they knew him. They had no idea who the real man was.

The man lifted his eyes off the lonely hearts ad and only saw one other man in the clandestine ace in the hole far away from the city and roads. Their last job had only been hours ago, and they needed to cool off before the next bank and mail heists in Kansas City. They had five weeks to wait things out. *One more goddamned month in hell with Beelzebub's minions.*

The Pinkertons had needed an agent to crack the confidence and trust of a band of outlaws, and Bart had sought him out for the impossible job with a nice pot of money attached. So now he was posing as a criminal, and using a dead man's name—a man he had arrested years before, when he was a sheriff. They spoke through the wanted ads. Amos delivered messages to Ada in the code they'd created months prior. This was a matter of life and death.

Now, this notice from Ada changed the game. He leaned into the chair and smirked, a small bit of joy coursing through him. Ada wasn't a real woman. It was a code that he used when talking to his deputies when he was wearing the white hat and on the right side of the law. Only one man—the one who put him on this job—knew how to reach him through the want ads of this paper.

The last message he sent was two months ago. Silence meant one of two things: either he had turned and forgotten his duty or he was dead. Bart was sending an SOS to his Pinkerton agent, and right then, Amos Tanner—former sheriff and Pinkerton agent to some, and Deadwood Dick to others—knew he had to get to Kansas City earlier and make amends to the Pinkerton boss.

Bart couldn't string a series of loving words together if he had a Colt pointed at his dome. The fine words belied seething anger. Deadwood understood. If one of his Pinkerton men had gone off the book and hadn't surfaced except for sightings and thefts, he would have felt the same way. Plans weren't predictions. If they were, Amos would be back in Oklahoma on his farm, living life in the boundaries of legitimacy and freedom, untethered to the Pinkerton Agency, his former boss, or the past undercover work he once did. But he was close to getting the answers, and the head of the crime ring, the agency wanted.

One more month, and he would have his serene life back. The man snorted at the idea of a clean, simple life. No Pinkerton agent made clean breaks from the agency. Traces of old cases haunted you. Debts and promises made to fellow agents were never forgotten and could always emerge from the shadows. A man saves your life, and he comes to you with a favor five years later. *I could have turned him away*, Amos thought. He knew that he couldn't. Pinkertons never gave up and never turned down a case.

Underneath Bart's note was another code. *9th and Central. Cut and shave special. D only.*

His gut roiled, and his jaw tightened. It was too soon. The gang was hot and on the lam. But the mastermind of the gang, the General, had made his move, as he'd promised, with the ad and the words. The next heist was ready to go, and the General had the final instructions.

The General had never seen a day of service to his country. Deadwood Dick called him that nickname in all of his reports to his

Pinkerton contact. He was an old criminal mastermind who kept several groups doing his bidding across the Western states. They were paid mercenaries, working to create havoc through simple grafting and complicated robberies and reaping the mastermind a fortune. Deadwood Dick reread the last line. *D only.* The old man only wanted to meet him, the unofficial chief of the crew.

A bit of joy broke through his dark mood. The Great Spirit was having mercy on him. He might be able to get this man to admit his evil deeds and finally be free of his debt to Bart.

Finally, free and able to press toward the new call on his life.

One of his posse members made coffee on the stove and was now attempting to fry the eggs that he'd stolen from a chicken coop a few miles back. A squeal from the other room, followed by the masculine rough words, grunting, and bedspring squeaks, told him that his other partners were still sharing the calico queen who let them live in her house in exchange for hard fucks and orgasms.

He hated all of this.

"You gonna do something today, Dick?" the man at the stove asked. Harry was the name his mama gave him after pushing him out, but the sour-faced man went by Buster. "Get off your ass with those books and do some man things?"

Once he was off his job, he was useless, unproductive, and of no use to the men around him. In fable, he lived up to that nickname. In truth, he was never parted from his job, intimately wrapped up in the lies and details of his life as a criminal.

He folded the newspaper and tucked it into his pocket. No one in here could read. They needed him to decipher codes and documents. Even if they didn't like him, they trusted him to do his job. "Kansas City is what, two hours away?"

"Yeah." Buster flipped the egg and beat it into a hard, sloppy mess. "We'll be there soon. Waiting to get the word to go."

"We got it." Deadwood Dick dropped a rock-hard biscuit into his pocket. Awful food and conditions would be alleviated once he got into the city. "I'm going to scout the location and get the instructions. We may have to move earlier than expected."

"I got time to poke her, right?" Buster jerked his thumb over his shoulder. The well-timed, well-faked moan of the whore punctured the house. "I get your turn too since you always turn down good cunt."

Deadwood Dick nodded, his face hard and stoic, before stuffing his hat on his head and heading out to check on his horse. It would take him a half a day to get there and find lodging and then another day to set up the drop and parlay messages to the General and Bart. These men on this crew were the worst of the money hungry, pussy chasing, and craven thieves he knew. They deserved whatever fate awaited them in Kansas City and beyond. He did, too. He hoped he would get his redemption sooner rather than later.

CHAPTER THREE

"Are you possessed by the Great Satan, yourself?"

Sunday dinner was a dedicated time of peace, as declared by Tamar's sister Priscilla, and today Priscilla's husband Charles Henderson, the only man in the family—and the town's richest black man—ignored those rules and launched into her.

"May I at least sit before you start lobbing insults?" Tamar slid into her seat next to Priscilla and bowed her head for a quick word of grace. *Dear Lord, help me to not kill this imbecile of a man with any of the available utensils on this finely set table.* She opened her eyes and spied the food she wanted. "Charles, please pass the green beans. Delilah, the roast chicken and rolls, please."

"What kept you away for so long, sister?" Delilah asked between bites and with a laugh in her eyes. Both older sisters shot her a look to be quiet.

"Another issue at the press."

"The damn place should be burnt to a crisp, if you ask me."

"No one asked you, Charles. The *Advocate* has been in our family for years."

"I am the head of this family now, and I know the history. Stop this foolishness before you get killed," Charles huffed in righteous anger.

He's like our own dragon, Tamar thought as she lifted a sliver of chicken to her plate. Her stomach thanked her for feeding it. She normally ignored her hunger for most of the day, going until she couldn't stop. "Not one person wants to kill me. They desire that I stop speaking the truth."

"No, the Klan wants you dead." Delilah passed the basket of rolls around the table. "Sorry, but I had to tell someone. I read that note."

"There is no Klan in Missouri," Charles said with vehemence coating his words. "The Klan doesn't exist. White and black are equal here."

"And what about the Indians who were here first before we crossed the Mississippi? Are they equal here?"

"I don't know about no red men, but I do know a fool put a rock through your window."

"It's a harmless prank. If I ran from a rock, I wouldn't be in business."

"First they come with rocks, and then fire and bullets," Priscilla said in a low, small voice. "We want you to live."

"I know *you* do." Tamar squeezed her sister's hand and swiveled to the red-faced man glaring at her. "But he would prefer to have me dead."

"Why can't you act like a lady? Quiet, submissive, and demure with no political thoughts. Women can't handle complicated ideas."

"Some men can't either," Delilah said, jumping up from the chair. "May I be excused? I would like to finish reading my Quintilian." She left without being dismissed, flouncing off to the library.

"That girl should know about cooking, sewing, and other woman things, not philosophy and economics."

"That girl is your sister-in-law. That girl is doing what we promised our parents and grandparents we would do. Go to school and become of use to the race. How quickly we forget that your dear wife went to school and has a noggin full of knowledge." Tamar squelched the rising tide of anger that wanted to roll off her tongue and shot a teeth-achingly sweet smile to her brother-in-law.

"You Freeman women … "

"Are the best thing that happened to you." Priscilla moved to her husband and kissed his forehead, while smoothing his coat lapel as if she was smoothing his ruffled feathers. "Take a cigar on the porch, my dear, while I get dessert."

Tamar and Priscilla watched the man stumble out of the dining room, mumbling about his hopes for dessert to be a mocha cake. Once he was gone, Tamar shushed her sister. "Don't say it."

"I just ask for peace one day out of the week. One ding-dong day for my family to come together."

"He's smoking on my porch. You know how much I hate smoke."

"This is our house, made by our grandfather and father. We all have a right to this house. You just happen to live here right now." Priscilla fixed all of the plates into a pile, the top dish loaded with refuse. "Can you please just be nice to him?"

"He attacked me first," Tamar said with a pout. She scooped a bit of the mashed potatoes out of the bowl and popped it in her mouth. "I only go after those who come for me."

"Charles has a point. It's too dangerous for you to write and publish the things you do."

"Daddy wrote the same things."

"Daddy was a man. You're a woman. You can't expect people to believe a colored woman has a place in the public square and is able to say all the things you're saying. Equal voting, lynching, civil rights ... you're talking like a mad woman with no hopes of ever getting married."

"I don't know if you're more concerned about my marital prospects or the death threats."

"I wish you wouldn't make light of things. If you had a family, maybe you wouldn't be so strident about that paper and trying to be martyr."

"I have a family. You and Delilah are Freemans like me."

"I meant a husband and some children. You must want that. Every woman does."

Every woman doesn't. The words fell off her tongue into the void of her mouth. Priscilla wouldn't understand the passion that drove her, the fear that she'd had when they left Tennessee, and the pride she felt when she made a small shift in opinion. *I want to be someone and let the world know who I am.* Her sister didn't have to fight for that; the world knew who she was when she opened her mouth to sing or when she stepped into the room.

"I want our race to be able to live and thrive, not just survive," Tamar said. "And I want the new edition of the paper to be ready for print Tuesday." Tamar rose from the table and tore into the soft yeast roll. She popped the bits into her mouth and savored the flavor. Her sister cooked just like their mother had.

"You can't leave. I have dessert. It's your favorite."

Not even lemon queen cake would entice her to sit with Charles for another minute. "Save one for me. The newspaper must be printed."

CHAPTER FOUR

Only three things were open in the dead of night: the doors of a saloon, a harlot's legs, and the publishing office for the *Kansas City Advocate.*

Or so Deadwood Dick had been told. The legs of an easy woman and the saloon he could guarantee because he'd just visited the saloon to clinch the details of the robbery with the team's contact. But the newspaper being open, hardly.

He prayed a silent prayer and crossed himself the way he'd learned at the boarding school he was forced to attend. Any and all help from the heavens was welcomed because Deadwood Dick must get this message to his beloved. He smiled at the subterfuge. Each week beneath their noses, his men read the lonely hearts, laughing at the poor suckers waiting around for some woman.

His woman—Ada—was waiting on him, and she was angrier than a hive of 10,000 hornets. Her last message told him so. The words burned in his mind.

I've lost hope. I think you have turned. I can't trust you.

"Never," he whispered. He was always faithful to Ada, the law, and his scruples. He had to let his contact—Ada, or in real life, a burly man who would have molly-whopped him for calling him that—know the truth and that the plan was still a go.

With all his musing and thinking, Deadwood Dick walked right to the publishing offices. He tested the doorknob, and it yielded under his grasp. The cluttered office was open, but no one was at the front desk. The office was quiet except for the angry hiss of a machine. The printing press, he assumed. "Hello there?" he said, easing through the door.

The cock of a gun greeted him, and a familiar sight—a gun muzzle—came into view as he rounded the corner. A small woman with a large gun was one of the things he avoided in life. The other, a pint-sized woman with a large gun.] He raised his hands to show he wasn't armed, and the first voice to break the quiet was the woman's voice. "My husband does not take kindly to strangers intruding on his wife," she said.

"I come in peace."

"At this late of night?" She eyed him suspiciously.

For an outlaw—or the men out to capture them—half past nine in the evening was hardly late. Things were barely getting warmed up at that time. "I promise. Your door was open."

She stepped out of the dark corner of the office, and he couldn't think for a moment. She was a pocket Venus with a true hourglass figure, clear skin, and huge dark-fringed eyes, along with a damn impressive steady hand to handle such a big weapon. "Not for you. And you are?"

Amos thought carefully to construct a response. The woman's looks stunned him into dumbness. "Ma'am, I would like to place a lonely hearts ad."

"You're late. You missed the deadline. And you didn't answer my question." The woman didn't lower her gun, but he watched her steadily assess him and the situation.

"I know, but I am hoping for a kind lady's grace."

"That kind lady isn't here. If you're here to rob me, know that I will shoot you when you leave."

"A coward shoots in a man's back."

The lady snorted. "I would shoot you in the front. Not trying to kill you, just leave you with a walking reminder not to mess with women."

"My apologies, madam. I'm in a bind and I am swinging through town. I need to make this notice. For a lady friend," he added.

"At this time of night?" The lady closed her eyes and shook her head. She was one of those types. Prim and proper with delicate sensibilities. What did he expect?

He dipped his head. "It's a message to confirm my fidelity for my intended."

Tamar rolled her eyes at him. That look and her sigh made him believe that she heard these lines before. "You have wild oats to sow, and I bet your intended knows that."

He shrugged and slowly moved his hands down to his pocket. "Hold on," he said, pulling a wad of bills out of his pocket and laying the stash on the counter. "I'm serious. I need to place the ad at any cost."

The money on the counter beckoned. He saw it in her eyes—the way they widened and then sparkled at the bounty before her. "Count it," he offered. He thought better of the offer and peeled off the bills. He counted each piece until he had fifty dollars laid out for her.

"You're making me a great offer, but I will have to reset the press."

"Triple that for your efforts." Her eyes widened to the size of pigeon's eggs. "You can buy a lot of pretty dresses for one hundred fifty dollars."

Her eyes narrowed, and he knew in an instant that he'd said the wrong thing. She was going to pump buckshots into him for offending her. "I'd rather buy my sister a ticket so she can go to Howard University to become trained in Latin and Greek. It's late, and I'm tired."

"I will stay with you until you finish. It is imperative that I get this want ad out to my Ada."

"Well, your beloved Ada certainly isn't concerned about her own fidelity. And Ada can wait a week," she said with a snort. "If she was top of your mind, you wouldn't have missed the submission deadline that appears in every paper."

The woman wasn't weak, but he'd known that before he met her. She had a backbone of steel and the mouth of a rabble-rouser. She wielded her opinions like a well-sharpened blade, slicing any man or woman not on the side of justice and right. *But she's still a woman.* He implored to what he had been warned was the touch point of the weaker sex: her heart. "Have you been in love before?"

She snickered. "Once when I caught a flu. I got over it. And I still don't know you. Tell me who you are."

Mentioning his name probably wouldn't endear her to him, but he wasn't looking for support or interest. He needed to get his message to Bart Quarles, his Pinkerton contact and the best lawman he ever had the privilege of working for.

He sighed before revealing the fake truth he'd created when he took on this duty. It usually didn't bother him, but with her, it stung like a bee's venom in a tender area. *Odd*, he thought. *What was it about this woman that makes me want to be honest?* The gun close to his face probably had much to do with his pinch of conscience. That and she looked like the lady he wanted to share his life with.

"I'm waiting two seconds," she said, waving her shotgun. "Before I shoot you between the eyes."

She would shoot him, and everything he'd worked for this far on this case and in his life would be for nothing. He'd die undercover as Deadwood Dick, and his body would never return to his beloved land in Oklahoma. *I can't give up now*, he thought. He closed his eyes and took a long inhale before answering with the name that still felt clunky on his lips. "Deadwood Dick at your service."

CHAPTER FIVE

Tamar lowered her weapon and eyed the man warily. The infamous Deadwood Dick was in her office. Sure, there were several of them in the lore of the Wild West. Only one was still in circulation, or so everyone thought. The lamps in her office gave the tall man a bronze glow, which was much different from the description of the Deadwood Dick she'd heard about. "Prove yourself," she said, barely getting the words out.

He rocked on his heels, thumbs hooked in his coat pockets. A hint of a devil-may-care smile teased his lips and changed the shape of his face. Instead of fearsome and rugged, he looked inviting and charming. He looked like a good time and trouble wrapped up in barbed wire. *Look, enjoy, but don't touch*, Tamar thought. She stared at his full lips, knowing he was saying something. His words hit her ears eventually. "Thieves don't carry passports with stamps for all their crimes," he said.

"Deadwood Dick stutters," she said evenly as she moved around the room still keeping an eye on the man. "And he is short. What are you, over six feet tall? Something's not right." Tamar knew her outlaws. "You aren't him. Reveal who you are or you will be taken out of here with a bullet hole in your precious body."

"You know that more than one of us exists. I will not harm you." He put his weapons on the counter where she could see them.

"You will leave here with a hot piece of lead in your body. I need proof."

"Draw your shades," he countered, leveling his gaze with hers and nodding to the windows. "And I will prove who I am to you."

She reached out and yanked the shades. The whirr of the shade dropping filled the office. "Done. Prove yourself."

Tamar saw a book sticking out of his coat pocket. "Hand me that book." He dutifully filled her request as he deposited the book on the counter. She flipped the book over. The Bible. A thief with a holy book? Wonders never cease. She opened the cover and scanned the first page. "Amos is your real name. Amos," she said, enjoying the crispness of the name on her tongue. The beautiful stranger had a real name. She wanted to press him for more details. Where was he from? Who were his people? What did he do? Who was he really? Was he married? Did he have children?

All of those questions were silenced when Amos nodded and pressed a finger to his lips. "Don't tell anyone," he said with a slight embarrassment. "No one wants to be robbed by an Amos. But you can trust an Amos."

Tamar snickered. The man had some humor and some guts, she thought as he casually waited for her as if it was a normal and everyday endeavor for a known bank robber to stand in a newspaper office with a spinster. Maybe it was for him. But this was out of the ordinary. Her days in the office consisted of debating about bills, writing columns, arguing with the respectable members of the community who thought she pushed too hard and was too radical, and setting type.

This was exciting, but she had a paper to put to bed. She had to put out the next week's issue with the newest Booker T. Washington speech. Tamar moved behind the counter, swiped the money into her apron pocket, and slapped a piece of paper and stub of a pencil on the counter. "Write your message."

He scribbled out the message and reread it twice. "Done," he said, extending it to her. Her hand shook as she accepted. "I'm not going to hurt you. Trust me, Tamar."

Jolted by his use of her name, she raised her head. Something about the way he said her name made it feel intimate. Her mind skittered around. She rarely heard a man call her anything but

Miss Freeman. And this impressive man calling her by her God-given first name caused her mind to go tumbling. "You know my name," she said with breathier softness than she desired.

"I do. Who doesn't know about the lady causing grief with her little newspaper?"

She rolled her eyes. "This operation isn't little. I have one of the largest circulations in Missouri and Kansas. I even have copies that go to the border to Oklahoma Territory."

"And you know my name," Amos also-known-as-Deadwood-Dick said.

"Yes, but who doesn't?"

Amos shrugged. He dropped his eyes to the rough-hewn countertop and spun the pencil stub between his fingers. "Half poppycock, half-truth. Don't believe everything you see in print," he said, avoiding her eyes.

Tamar watched him. She knew men who were liars, and he was doing the classic liar maneuvers of not looking her in the eye. She pressed on with her questions the way a good journalist would. "But you are a robber like Robin Hood?"

"There's no proof such a man ever existed. But I won't deny you are an outlaw."

"I beg your pardon. What—" Tamar asked with huffing defiance, her grip on the weapon loosening. He took advantage of her righteous anger and slight pause. He grabbed the gun out of her slackened grip and spun her around in one quick maneuver. Before she knew it, her back was nestled against his hard, very hot body. She resisted, struggling against his vice-like grip.

"Don't fight me, Tamar. It only makes things harder," he said in a whisper that caressed her ear. His words silenced her as the reality of his words set in.

"What things are harder, mister?" she asked.

"You have a lot to learn, Miss Tamar." He laughed, a gentle chuckle that pulsed with desire and humor. "And I wish I could teach you."

"You are incorrigible and a thief. Let me go," she said with a fierce determination that did not betray the part of her that wanted him to continue to hold her and press his body against hers.

"Not yet," he said. He rested his head on the curve of her neck and inhaled deeply before kissing the shell of her ear. "I shouldn't do that."

"You should not." Tamar faltered to find the words. One minute, the man had her bristling in anger. The next, she was wrapped in his arms, blazing with desire and want and ready to beg him for more kisses. "You are a horrible man to keep me this way."

"I am," he said with a heavy, tortured sigh. He put an inch of distance between them, and she missed the tight connection they shared. "I am a bad man. Now would an outlaw allow himself to be called those things and take no retribution? You should be more careful with that counter and at whom you point your weapon."

Tamar thinned her lips and shook her head with vigor. "I don't work under the threat of a gun held by any man, including you."

"This is not a threat. I'm preventing my own murder by merely holding your weapon. You shall receive it back when we are completed. Now will you do what I asked?"

"I don't help outlaws, thieves, or gamblers."

"Only harlots and the brokenhearted can receive your help? I am only interested in your printing press. I have no other interest in you. I am a desperate man, but not so desperate to take advantage of a woman."

"You and every other man in the damnable state have no interest in me," she muttered.

"Don't compare me to any other man. I have a vested interest in you, Miss Tamar. Will you help me?"

Tamar shivered. The man knew how to coat his words with honey and clover so they would be appealing and easier to swallow.

"I shall do this under duress. Your ad will run in the morning, I promise."

He let her go, slipping his arm from around her. "Here," he said, pulling a slip of paper from his pocket. "This is the message I need to send."

"This ad is nonsensical," she said, drawing his attention away from her. "I'm still true. Still faithful. Still on the straight and narrow."

"Everything between lovers may not make sense." He stilled her hand. "You're not going to change the writing. It must run as is."

"No, we run what you request. You forgot one part." She snatched a pencil and started to scribble. "Who is the lovely lady on the receiving end of this?"

He walked to the door, pocketing her weapon. "I follow up on any promise made to me. I will be back."

"May I have my gun?"

"Tomorrow or later," he said with a nod. "We both have something to look forward to. And the woman's name is Ada." Then she watched him disappear into the night.

CHAPTER SIX

If Tamar wasn't so mad about losing her gun and having to do a new press run, she would have jumped the outlaw's bones. She realized that in the early morning as she pushed out the new copies, handed them to her delivery boys, and staggered to her house. She fell into bed, still clothed in her ink-streaked gown, and had restless dreams about kissing and touching the man known as Deadwood Dick.

"It is enough to make a woman go mad," Tamar huffed now into the silence of the back room of the newspaper. Even after she'd woken up, her imagination had continued to work, filling in the gaps of her conversations and thoughts with images of his lips and his hands caressing her. A woman like her should not entertain any thoughts about these things. Her right mind knew that, but the desire, long trapped underneath logic and activism, had sparked to life. *What am I going to do with that, and with whom? That outlaw isn't coming back.*

A hard thump jolted Tamar out of her contemplations. She turned to see Delilah hovering in the doorway. The glowing smile her sister normally carried was replaced with a somber glower. "Lazy bones, you have a crowd awaiting your presence. They've been waiting for two hours. Where have you been? You usually wake up with the roosters."

Tamar hid her embarrassment with the drop of her head, her eyes focused on her shoes. One interaction with a handsome fugitive, and she was acting like a lovesick woman who lacked common decency and common sense. "Who has whipped up such a tizzy in my office?" she asked, brushing past her sister.

Delilah grunted. "That man who came in yesterday. He's been here since I opened."

Tamar's heart skipped five beats. She swirled around the room, searching for the mirror. How did she look? All this concern for an outlaw, she thought, hastening to the front of the office. The delight on her face melted away when she caught a glimpse of the man waiting for her. It wasn't the outlaw. It was the Herculean-sized Pinkerton agent with the broken heart.

Bart nodded at her. "Good morning, miss. Clearly, I'm not who you expected."

"Certainly, you are." The lie tasted like rust on her tongue. Bart *wasn't* the man she was hoping for. "It's a pleasure to see you again, although all is well here. No sign of troublesome meddlers who hate my work."

"Yet. The day and the week are still early."

"It must be horrible to see trouble and criminality at every turn."

"It's my job, ma'am." Bart slapped the day's paper on the counter and pointed to the ad encircled in red pencil. "Just like this is my job. Who submitted this?"

Delilah snatched the copy and read the ad aloud. "I guess Ada has her choice of suitors."

The man cut his eyes sharply, his fingers rolling a cigar tightly before shoving it into his mouth. "I know. I don't take kindly to another man intruding on my affections."

"And unfortunately, we cannot disclose the name of the man who wrote these notes. It's private."

"So it was another man," Delilah said in a hushed voice. "You have competition."

"Delilah, hush." Tamar swatted her sister on the bottom and pushed her to the desk. "She has an overactive imagination and too much time on her hands. Man or woman, I cannot tell you who wrote that. Our submitters require secrecy, and we hold that in high regard."

"This is a police matter."

"And you are not the police. Pinkertons haven't been sworn into duty or action here in Kansas City."

"Ma'am, let me make this clear and polite. I need the name of the man who submitted this. Do the community a favor and take this menace to society off the streets."

"You assume that you know who he is."

"I have an idea. An outlaw charmer who has vile intentions."

"He is not vile. He is a gentleman. Amos. That is all I can tell you."

"Amos?" The large man stroked his chin. "Amos. Tell me a last name. I can have you arrested for impeding an investigation."

"You cannot arrest me. You have no right."

"I have all the right in the world." He placed his badge on the table and leaned onto the countertop. His impressive bulk cast a shadow on her, and his silence was meant to intimidate and frighten.

"You've practiced this, haven't you?" she said, a slight smile tipping her lips. "I'm not afraid of you."

"I am a Pinkerton, but I am still a sheriff in this state. I can create jurisdiction and cause all types of headaches for you and the smart one."

Tamar's body tightened at the threat. "Leave Delilah out of this."

"I will," Bart said with a steely edge. "All you have to do is give me the slip he used to write out his notice. Otherwise, your hopes for your sister to go to Howard and become an asset to the race will vanish."

Tamar studied the badge and the thinly veiled threat before sliding open the counter drawer. Out of the clutter popped the most recent notices. She rummaged through the drawer until she found the familiar handwriting and name. "Happy now?" she asked, slamming it on the counter.

The man nodded in appreciation before tucking the slip into his jacket pocket. "I understand your anger. Does he visit often?"

"No."

"I assume he will be back since payment was not rendered. May I leave a response to the person who wrote this?"

"You have a tendency to do what you want."

Bart smiled widely, revealing a gap in his teeth. He could have been a gorgeous man if he smiled more and threatened less. "I do. I certainly do," he said, opening his vest and placing a bullet on the desk. "This is for him."

"A bullet? What does this mean?" she said, picking up the object and scrutinizing it.

"It will be the bullet that I put in him if he does not follow my wishes." With a solemn nod, he left the building. Tamar pocketed the bullet, an icy shiver of terror running through her veins. She was now mixed up in dangerous business.

• • •

Amos entered the *Advocate* office and placed Tamar's gun on the counter.

"You again." She closed her book and put it to the side before glancing at him. "If you knew better, you would stay away."

"If I knew better, I wouldn't have come here at all. I came to return this to you."

"Thank you. I never thought I would see her again."

"You can't have it until you make a promise. You won't turn this gun on me again."

She nodded. "Accepted. I won't. May I?"

Amos passed the gun to Tamar. He avoided her question but not her gaze. He looked directly at her when he spoke this time. "Is this husband of yours coming through this evening?"

"My husband is a fiction," Tamar said, noting how his shoulders fell, the deepness of his eyes, as they were intent on her, and his wide, pillow-soft lips. "But people will be stopping in to see me." She maintained late hours and had few people stop in during the day—and even fewer in the evening. Her sisters were occupied, Priscilla with her husband and Delilah with her correspondence studies, and she doubted either would check up on her.

He moved around the counter to where she stood. "How does this work?" he asked, pointing to the printer resting in the corner.

"It's temperamental at times. And this—" She hit the machine. "This is one of those nights where Old Bertha decides what she will and will not do for me."

"Do you mind?" he said as he headed to the printer.

Tamar sifted through the contents of her mail, seeking one last letter to the editor. The majority of the letters were for farmers looking for field hands, and single women—the never married, widows, and divorcees—seeking a man to till the soil and warm their beds. The lonely want ads gave her a boost in revenue, and she saved those in a pile for her sister, the resident matchmaker who, thanks to her diligent efforts and love-addled brain, had created ten marriages, a few discreet clandestine relationships, one divorce, and four babies. Politics and the upliftment of the race were Tamar's issues, always featured prominently in the issue. The biggest story thus far was her opinion on the lawlessness of the West and the men (and a few women) behind it. Checking her running total, she had four people who agreed with her and no disavowals.

"I don't agree with you," he said, staring at the piece of equipment. "She is feisty, but you need to warm her up a bit."

Tamar puffed out an exasperated gush of air. "I guess you have practice with ornery women."

"Cantankerous horses, yes. I prefer my lady friends to be compliant and yielding." He turned back to the machine and slowly toyed with the gears. "Let her rest a bit. I'm sure you worked the heck out of her tonight," he said, his eyes trailing over to the pile of freshly printed papers.

"If you ever want to renege on a life of crime you are more than welcome to work here and fix this hunk of metal by talking to her."

"Is that a guarantee, Miss Tamar?"

Her cheeks flushed with the thought of him fixing many other things in her life. If anyone could read her lusty thoughts right now, she would be doused in holy water, submerged in holy oil, and prayed over for a fortnight. "I was making light. Joshing you. A joke."

"I don't hear many of those. I don't have many things that brighten my day or outlook."

"I can give you plenty." She scrambled to her desk and pulled open some drawers. A joke book. She thumbed through the book. "Why is a dog like a tree?"

He shook his head. "No clue."

"Because they both lose their bark once they're dead." She giggled and tossed the book at him. "Come on, that was funny."

A slight grin cracked his face and struck her dumb. The man was stunning. His face completely changed with the simple tilt of his lips. Could men be stunning? "You tell me one."

Amos combed through the pages, absorbed in the assorted jokes, and she took her time to soak him in. His head popped up, and she jolted out of her daze. "Found one. What is the best way to keep a man's love?"

Tamar shrugged. "How?"

"Not to return it," Amos answered. "That actually is true."

"I can't believe that. Love should be equal on both sides. What do you think?"

"Tamar, you have given me more entertainment than I have had in a long time."

"Then you, sir, should get out more."

"How can I repay you?

She broke the spell by stepping back into reality and away from him. A few inches closer and she would have been in his arms, against that broad chest, and … Tamar touched her lips. She could have kissed him. Her first kiss ever. *Stop this madness*, her mind warned. *He's a strange man who popped up in the dead of night to craft a love note to a woman who didn't want him.* Tamar caught sight of the concerned look on his face. "You fixed Old Bertha. That is enough. We have to run copies in the morning but I can start on this tonight. Your ad will be printed. I'm sure Ada will be pleased to hear from you. But, sir, know that this is no way to court a woman, even the ones on the farm."

He grinned, and the glow of his smile warmed her across the room. "You have a lot of opinions. And I'm not courting her. I already have her intense interest."

"If you desire to keep her intense interest, take Dear Priscilla's advice. Write her a letter."

"When I want your advice about wooing, I will ask."

"I'm sure you don't need any advice. You probably have a trail of broken hearts and lifted skirts. You can always expand your repertoire."

"Pray tell me. How do you woo a woman?"

"Letters," she blurted out. "The want ads are no place to woo a woman. But a finely crafted letter can create worlds that only exist between lovers. They can open hearts and if necessary part locked knees."

He grinned. "And I'd write about … ?" He trailed off. "My life is hardly noteworthy."

"In the beginning write about things that draw you to her. Don't frighten her." Tamar tossed her hands up in frustration.

"I am no good with this. You should write a letter to our Dear Priscilla column."

"Is there a real Priscilla?"

She nodded. "My dear sister who just married a dolt wrote it. Now I am responsible until I find a new columnist since her husband wants her to focus solely on her house and child rearing."

"You don't think highly of your brother-in-law."

"Men who need to boast and brag about every minuscule accomplishment are making up for another shortfall on their lives." Her gaze dropped. "I'm sure you don't have that issue.

"The need to compensate for lack? Not quite. You've been a witness to that."

She moved away quickly, breaking eye contact with him. "My brother-in-law is in cahoots with every politician and ne'er do well. He hates what I do."

"Publishing a paper?"

"Telling the truth and shaming the devils that take advantage of others." Her eyes burned bright, thinking of the change her words had created. "We have to do better, and I ask people to do that."

"How can I repay you for your graciousness and generosity?"

"I want to know the story from your lips."

"There's not much to tell. A man who tread down the wrong path with little hope of redemption."

"If you believe in that," she thumped on the cracked, dusty, and worn Bible, "you must know that there is grace and hope for every sinner who falls short."

"You say that like you don't believe."

"I haven't had much to sin for and I never witness miracles. I believe what I know and what I see. Things that can be proven. I didn't believe in you, and now I do because proof is in the flesh before me."

"And you want more?"

"Always. You have a story that should be told."

"There's no story."

"I will pay you."

"I reckon not. I'm not for sale. Create a new story for me. Everyone else has added to my infamy."

"Fame and infamy, bah. I'm trying to find out why the most famous robber wants to be anonymous and unknown, hiding behind fables and lore."

"The same reason you do. It's easier to pretend and be someone else."

"I am not hiding."

"You write. You publish. Do you ever travel? See the world?"

"It's hard to do those things when you have a paper—and a duty to the race."

"That doesn't preclude you from fun and excitement. Or to be alone just you and your love with the stars and bluebells as your blanket and mat."

"You make life on the run sound romantic. It's easy to forget you are a criminal."

"That's not the sum of who I am. I can shed that identity if I desire."

"Why do you keep it?"

"One day, I will tell you as Tamar, the woman, not the T. Freeman, the publisher of the *Advocate*."

"And who will tell me this story? Deadwood Dick or Amos?"

"Amos. A story for a story."

She sat at the desk, a pencil tucked in her grip and poised above a stack of paper. She was ready to scratch his truths and lies into a permanent state. "Start. You go first."

"I need a question to prompt me."

"Who is Ada?"

"You still don't believe me."

"I know she's not your affianced or your mama. Your face—you try to make it a mask, but mischief plays at your lips."

He rubbed his lower lip. Her eyes followed the movement, taking in the curve of his large hand and the plush contours of his mouth. Never had a man's lips or hands fascinated her so. She ached to feel the weight of his hands and mouth on her at the same time, the pressure of them guiding her to act out the wanton, traitorous desires coursing through her.

"Things get blurry when I'm with you," Amos said. "I've told a lot of lies, and a woman like you makes a man like me lose the breadcrumb trail he left to remember his lies."

"You cannot try your flirtations on a journalist. I will dig out the veracity and sincerity of any statement."

"You are more than a writer and fact checker. Don't be humble about your sublime beauty."

Sublime? She jotted that on her paper as a reminder to check that word. It sounded bad, but the look on his face told her it wasn't. "Mighty words for a woman you just met." His brawn matched or exceeded his brain. She felt a push to know more from this stranger.

"When you get to be my age, you know when to say those things at the right moment. The spirit moved me to say it."

"Your spirit should stop being fresh."

"*For God's sake, hold your tongue and let me love.*" He grinned as she stared at him, trying to decipher the mountain of man in her presence. "Donne. Infatuation," he answered. "He's not a popular poet, but I enjoy his words."

She made another note on the sheet and hoped her sister had a volume of this Donne. "I don't read poetry. It seems superfluous in this world."

"It makes life beautiful; a few words distill a lot of truths."

"Truth is, it's early to declare your love for a woman you've encountered in the span of a day."

"I know your work. I've heard about you. If I were a good man with an honest life and a solid, honest job, I would have proposed when I walked in here."

"Like every other suitor, you would have been rejected. I don't entertain foolishness, requests for my submission, orders for my money, or demands that I give up my life and submerge into theirs."

"I would never ask that." He glanced out of the window and checked the time on his pocket watch. "It's getting late. How are you getting home?"

"With these," she said, kicking up her feet. "I stay close, and I walk between home and this office all the time."

"You won't tonight. When you are ready to leave, permit me to walk you home."

She bristled and set cold eyes and firm voice on him. "And the other nights you aren't here, what shall I do? Leave me in peace and do whatever it is that outlaws do at this time of night."

He gave up no hints, just a soft smile that hinted at the pleasure he felt. "I would like to walk you home." His voice was steadfast, his promise to protect her in the moment assured. A frisson of heat wound through her circulatory system at a rapid, dizzying speed.

"This is home for the moment." She turned to face him, the joy and tension etched on her face hidden in the shadows. "The Klan has threatened my house and office."

His jaw clenched so tightly she was afraid he would pop it out of place. "They will leave you alone, I promise."

"I don't take the promises of any man seriously," Tamar said. "The police have said the same thing, and nothing has changed. The threats still come."

The words died on his lips when the glass shattered. "Down," he yelled, tackling her and tucking her into his embrace.

"It's just another rock."

But it wasn't. Bullets whizzed through the air, lodging into the solid surfaces around them. "Those are not rocks."

"I am an American citizen under siege. I need my gun."

"No, stay still." He clamped his arms tightly around her waist, molding against his chest. "And quiet."

After the last round of bullets, horses galloped away, and the air of quiet descended upon them. Their breaths echoed in her ears, her heart racing as if it would never stop. The weight of it all came crashing down on her. "I could have died," she said, choking back a sob.

"You wouldn't have, Tamar. I promise you that." He stroked her hair and pressed her deeper into his embrace. He whispered words of comfort, and she listened to the deep, rumbling vibrations in his chest. Never had she been this vulnerable since her parents were alive and were there to make her pains and slights vanish. Never had she felt so comfortable and protected. She didn't want this cocooning solace around Amos to end.

Heavy footsteps charged up to the door and kicked it open. A familiar masculine voice broke through the murmurs. "Miss Freeman?"

"I'm right here," she answered, scrambling out of Amos's arms and confronting Bart, the lovelorn Pinkerton agent. "I'm fine, I promise. Tonight I was lucky."

Bart squinted, his eyes taking stock of the entire office now in disarray. "Are you sure? They lit up this place. Next time, it won't be a rock or bullets. It will be fire. Maybe a noose."

"She's fine." Amos rose from the floor and appeared at her side. "There's no need to scare the lady, sir."

The two men eyed each other warily, assessing each other with respect and suspicion. "And you are?" Bart asked.

"He's a friend."

"I've never seen you around these parts."

"I'm visiting. On my way to see my lady, Ada. It was late, and I decided to stop in to see my friend. I'm glad I did. Are you the law?"

"No, this man is a Pinkerton agent who came to see me yesterday. Before then, I never knew a kind Pinkerton existed—or that so many women named Ada existed." Her hands shook as she reached for the door. "I'm going to get the—"

"You're not going anywhere alone at this time of night. I will escort—"

"I can walk across the street." Tamar froze, a flash of fear washing across her entire body. Amos followed her gaze to the empty desk, stacked with science books and scribbled notes. "Oh my god. Delilah. She was supposed to be here tonight with me, but I left her."

"She's safe and sound. I have eyes on your place. As a matter of fact, Mr. Davis there," Bart said, nodding at the man on the door. "I believe you know him from your church. He can walk you home."

Tamar hesitated, her eyes sweeping the chaos of her once-orderly operation. The acrid and sour smell of gunpowder and the charcoal scent of gun smoke filled her lungs. Glass shards littered the floor and were now being ground into dust and fine particles by the men trampling through her offices. A muscle flicked angrily in her jaw when she saw the bullet holes puckering the walls. Her beloved printer had taken a hit or two from the barrage of gunfire. She stepped forward to get a closer look, and Bart intercepted her, his hand softly cuffing her arm.

"But this has to get cleaned up. I have to make this right," she said, a softness in her voice.

Bart tilted his brow, looking at her with uncertainty and sympathy. "I know, but you're shaken up. I, along with your friend here, will take care of it. Trust us."

Amos nodded in agreement. "Tamar, go. I will handle this for you. You can trust me."

"You can trust us," Bart countered, glaring at the other man. He released her and signaled to his man Davis to escort her home.

Tamar walked to the door and pirouetted back to face them. "Will I see you again?" she asked, staring directly at Amos. "I should properly thank you for saving me tonight."

Amos's expression stilled and grew serious. "Yes, ma'am, I will be calling on you very soon. You still have to get my story," he said before she walked out of the gun smoke and damaged office. "I promise."

• • •

After Tamar left, Amos stared at the door for the longest time, unsure what he'd just agreed to.

He turned to face Bart Quarles, who motioned for him to follow into the darker recesses of the office. Like a good employee, Amos followed. "You're a helluva man to catch up to, boss." He extended his hand to the large man standing at the edge of the office.

Bart raised his fist and clocked Amos with all his might. The blow landed square on his jaw. Amos stumbled a bit. His first reaction was to charge and hammer Bart. But he knew better. He deserved this hit for remaining mute for two months and not checking in with Bart, and taking a look at the man, he resisted his urge to battle him with fisticuffs. Bart still had a good fifty pounds of muscle and another four inches in height.

Amos tilted his head and took in the sight before him. "Hello works better than fists."

Bart shook his hand and grimaced. "Damn you, Tanner, and your iron jaw. It's been five months since I've seen hide or tail of you. I thought they turned you."

Amos shook his head. Never. Outlaws violated every instinct and moral he had. The few he did respect were doing these jobs for reasons bigger than a score. "I sent messages when I could. You received word when necessary."

"Not often enough," Bart said, pulling out a cigar and lighting it. Amos noted the move, one of Bart's nervous habits. His handler didn't show concern in the expected ways. "You pulled a major disappearing act and almost put everything in jeopardy."

"I'm still your man, boss."

Bart frowned, puffing smoke rings into the air. "The other two men I had said that. Then they turned and I had to put bullets in them."

"I'm not them."

"I know, I know." Bart yanked the cigar from his mouth and scowled. "And those ads in the *Advocate*—brilliant way to communicate. You write like a man who went to Lincoln or Howard," he said before pulling a long drag on the cigar.

Amos ducked his head. He was self-taught and read like a demon. He always had a book in his saddlebag. Now it was *Treasure Island* by Stevenson he'd lifted off a robbery and once finished he fully intended to return it with the rest of the stash he received. It wasn't his; he had no rights to keep it.

"You almost tipped off the lady publisher. Two men declaring their intentions for an Ada of Topeka."

"Shit, I don't care if I made the Almighty angry. I had to reach out again. They don't take too kindly to traitors or lawmen."

And I am both, Amos thought. The price of his double-dealing would be high. Death and torture. He had seen the evidence of spies in the military and as a lawman, prayed over their bodies, and put them into unmarked graves. He wasn't going to die like that. "They don't suspect anything."

"Don't go see a lady in this shape." Bart tossed him a satchel. Amos caught the satchel and looked inside. He needed to clean up. He looked up to see his boss smiling at him. In all his years of working undercover with him, Amos couldn't remember one time where his boss smiled.

The stoic lawman tilted his head. "What do you have for me?"

"My last operative report for the agency. The set-up is ready for you."

"They're still planning to rob the train—"

"At noon next Tuesday. I suspect that you'll be on the train."

"Do they suspect—"

Amos shook his head. "They suspect nothing. They know I went to visit a lady friend, and they assume I will be there all night and through the mid-day."

Bart narrowed his eyes, uncertain if he could trust the words. "It's your established pattern with them. And they don't get suspicious?"

"No," Amos answered with certainty. He had established the pattern with the gang. Instead of staying with them before a heist, he made a point to go out and away, discussing the women he had in the area. Seeing his women and flipping skirts were his good luck charm. And he had given them enough good luck on the road. They indulged him, cheered him on. But there were no women. "They will be riding in tomorrow. I'm coming later. We stay all over the city, never together in the same place."

"That was hardly what I expected."

"Plans changed. They suspected a traitor in the group."

"Not you?"

"Not even close. I'm the baddest man this side of the Mississippi." The myth of Deadwood Dick allowed anyone to bear that mantle. The exploits of his thieving and crimes carried far and wide.

"Your work here is done."

"Soon."

"You need to get some rest. I can—"

"No need. I have a woman to see."

"I warned you about the women and the job."

"I'm leaving duty soon."

"You never broke your duty for a skirt before."

Amos's jaw tightened, and he flexed his hand into and out of a fist. It was hard to keep from launching off and pummeling his handler. Otherwise, he would have hit Bart square in his face, breaking his hand and Pinkerton protocol. Tamar was more than a piece of tail, an easy tramp whose skirts he could flip for a dime and dance and without a care.

"Your response tells me she is a special thing." Bart either took everything in or had a third sense. Amos didn't want to know. "You have romantic intentions toward her."

"I kindly suggest you stop talking, Bart."

"A great many lawmen have been brought down by … " Bart considered his words when he caught the menacing look on Amos's face. "A woman."

"She's not like any other."

Bart snorted. "They are all the same. You'll break her heart."

"She could break mine."

"With what you are going to do, you're going to hurt her." The subtle message wrapped inside the words was *Don't go. Leave her alone.* "If you love her … you will stay away from her."

"Spoken from experience?"

Bart grunted. "You're not a man built for love and that sentimental malarkey. I know my kind. We catch bad men. We're lawmen."

"I was a lawman. I'm now an outlaw. And soon—"

"You'll be back to what you've always wanted. Don't forget your responsibilities. I need you to finish this out." Bart handed him the reins of the horse and buggy. "All the supplies your crew needs for the job. We can't afford to miss this opportunity."

"I want to get back to my life."

"You will once this is done. I will never ask you to step into this role again. It costs us to do this work," Bart said, his voice ringing with command. "Bring me those thieves and you can have your life back."

CHAPTER SEVEN

Amos stood at the back alley of the address the General gave him. Today he was dressed proper in a suit and tie, a hat low over his eyes. He could fade into the street, moving along with the other men who worked real jobs and had dull lives.

This spot was the finest barbershop this side of the Mississippi. Newspapers—even the *Advocate*—talked about the glorious accommodations: the mahogany-and-plate glass doors, the sparkling white ceramic tile, and the dark green Spanish leather custom barber chairs. Everything was the finest that could be procured in the open market.

Not that Amos would be able to make those reports. He was standing outside the entrance for deliveries and colored men. At the appointed time, the back door opened, and a fair-skinned man with blue eyes opened the door and eyed him from head to toe.

"We don't cut colored men here," the man said. "You can go to the shop off Troost Avenue. Same quality barbers and cheaper price."

Jim Crow laws forbade black and white men to get cut with the same blade. The barber before him couldn't get a cut in his own chair.

"Is this your place?"

"No, the owner's inside. Charles Henderson."

The name rang a faint bell in his head. There was a connection to Charles and the paper. Off the top of his head, he couldn't remember, and he couldn't waste time deciphering the clues. He had to get additional information. "There is a man getting a shave from Charles. He sent for me."

The man eyed him with a deep suspicion, but opened the door wider. "Wait here. I will ask."

Minutes later, Amos heard the heavy clump of footsteps toward the back. The barber who originally came was replaced with a fair-skinned, portly, and hazel-eyed man wearing a barbering coat. This must be the owner Charles. Whoever he was, the man's heated, venomous gaze pierced through Amos.

"Who are you to come into my place of business and demand to see an alderman?"

"I was asked to be here by a client who was getting his shave. I am following instructions."

"You do not ask for a man of his stature."

Amos squared up with certainty that this exchange would end with blows. "How do you know what I am?"

"Yes, he can. Sorry, Charles." Another man with a cape and a half-shaven face walked into the room. "Let me handle this."

"Your kind of rabble-rouser is not welcome here. You do this city and the community no justice," Charles said before turning on his heel.

"Excuse him. It's a pleasure to finally meet the man who is making me rich."

Amos nodded. "Same here." It was a pleasure to finally lay eyes on the man who was giving them orders. The confirmation that the ringleader was one of the state's finest politicians would be noted and given to Bart soon. "Mr. Aldus Miller."

"Let's not use names, shall we?" The man smiled, but the touch of humor didn't reach his cold eyes. "Here are the orders and what needs to happen."

"And after this?"

"This is the last one for some time. People are getting suspicious. You wait to hear from me again."

"Noted, boss."

The man clapped him on his back and shoved him out of the door. "Make me proud and make me rich, boy." Those were the last words he heard before the slamming of the door. Deadwood Dick received his orders for the last heist of the gang.

. . .

A dark shadow cast over her desk, and the man spoke with a bold conviction only a few snifters of brandy could give. "You must stop this," he said, leaning over her. "Tamar, this is not good for the family."

Tamar looked up from the stack of telegrams with determination lining her face. No one told her what to do or how to do anything with her paper. That no one included the man who charged into her office telling her to stop what she did best. Her sometimes idiotic brother-in-law was pacing the length of the small office and slapping a rolled-up edition of the *Advocate* against his palm.

Charles cleared his throat and repeated himself. "You must stop this cavorting with criminals."

Tamar puffed out an exasperated sigh. "I do not gallivant, and unlike others in this conversation, I do not associate with criminals." *Well, that was a lie.* She did associate with Deadwood Dick, more often than she should and not as often as her libido wanted. "Is that a new copy?" she asked, snatching the paper from him. She unfurled it and sighed. It was the latest edition. The fresh ink smudged. The copy was no good for delivery. She would have to print another one.

"You have to stop this," Charles said, clapping his hands together and still pacing. She could see his nerves were on edge. As the best barber—colored, white, or other—in the city, he had access to the city's leaders, all of whom hated the paper and by extension, Tamar.

"Stop what, Charles?" Tamar was annoyed. Her printing was ruined. *I should print again, but not tonight,* she thought looking at the testy machine that huffed and puffed its last breath just as she squeezed the last edition out. Possibly she could give this paper to the good reverend across the street at Allen Chapel AME. Reverend Turner didn't read the paper anyway; he only had the subscription to support the Freemans, one of the oldest families in the church.

Charles huffed. "These opinions are putting all of us in danger. Everyone is not as foolish as you."

Delilah stuck her head into the room. The obvious argument drew her interest like a bear to a honeycomb; the girl enjoyed debate more than anything else in the world. "We are not foolish. Tamar is the smartest and bravest person you know. Just because you don't have a steel backbone and corset like she does—"

"Thank you, Delilah. Get back to your studies." Tamar cut off her sister. Nothing would benefit them by pissing off their sister's husband. She turned back to the incensed Charles. "You know we Freeman women have a lot of spunk."

"That spunk will kill you if you aren't careful. The men that I know, I hear what they say about that troublesome woman. You are a thorn in the side of Kansas City for this … " He trailed off, shaking the paper in his hands and prowling around the office.

Hyperbole and verging on a jeremiad, Tamar thought. The man fuming in her office may not know the words, but he speechified like a professional in a bully pulpit. "I am doing my job as publisher of the paper my grandfather started."

"Our grandfather," Delilah corrected from the other room.

Charles fussed with the damaged newspaper, rifling through the pages until he reached the middle spread. "This foolishness," he said, pointing to the letters to the editor. "And you cannot keep giving the criminal element space to detail their operations."

"This criminal element! What in heaven's name are you talking about?" Tamar asked, astonishment filling her voice. "You must mean the governor, not anyone who writes for my paper."

Charles's nut-brown skin turned redder. He reminded Tamar of a kettle on a hot stove: if he got any madder, steam would whistle out of his ears. "You know who I mean. Criminals are using your paper to pass information back and forth. Oh, woman who knows everything, have you not seen the codes?"

"Prove it." She slammed the paper down. "Show me that you're not just talking crazy and wasting my time."

Charles flipped to the lonely-hearts section and pointed to an ad. "That one. That's what brought a dangerous man to see a fine, reputable client today."

Tamar snickered. Only Charles thought that Aldus Miller, the local alderman that the political machine pushed onto the populace, was a well-thought-of man. "Your client is a corrupt fiend," she muttered, reading the ad. It was an ad next to the ones she'd published for Amos and the Pinkerton agent. The content of the ad was not suspicious: Robert—Lola has a bolt of cloth for your new pants. Come to Gumbel Building *543, 10 sharp. "It appears to my intellectual mind that this Lola likes sewing and hates to wait. How do you know that it was this ad?"

"It is the address for my place of business with the right day and time." Charles huffed. "Connect the dots. Your newspaper is rife with chaos and criminality."

"It is my newspaper." Tamar glanced around the office that held two desks and a printing press. Had she and the paper been used for criminal acts? She'd considered these lonely hearts ads as a moneymaker, not an opportunity for mischief. She would worry about that later. Now she needed to dispatch Charles. "I own everything in here, and I have the right to publish what I see fit. That's what you fought for in the war."

In a normal conversation, Charles lit up when talking about his time during the Great War with the colored infantry and protecting the Union. Tonight was not one of those times. "And you have done a great work, detailing the lives and needs of our people in this state. But you are putting everything at risk by associating with this filth, these corrupt ideas, and your radical ideals." Charles punctuated his statement with a huff and the toss of the coiled up paper across the room. "Do you know these men who come to purchase space from you?"

Tamar flushed and busied herself with reorganizing her desk as to avoid his intent gaze. She knew a few of them, but only one made her wet with desire. She could tell Charles the truth that she was besotted with a younger man who was a thief. But that would bring too many questions. How did she know him? What was a good, honest businesswoman doing with the likes of him? Had she lost her mind?

She could hardly believe that she had known this man for the length of time it took to bat an eye. He'd inspired her very recent, very pleasant dreams.

Incredibly pleasant dreams.

Tamar crossed her arms over her chest and stood her ground. "Who put you up to this?"

Charles grimaced. "I can speak on my own."

His motivations weren't pure. Probably the mayor who hated her questioning of his budget and his segregationist policies. Charles had no problems before with the paper. Why now?

"The First Amendment of the United Constitution, which you so vigorously defended in the military, gives me and any other journalist freedom of speech." Tamar stamped over to the corner and unfurled the battered copy Charles had tossed about. "I'm talking about the new election laws that are silencing our votes and are upending the gains made since Reconstruction."

Charles snatched the copy away and vigorously read the column, his lips moving over each word. "You're causing upheaval, speaking about things you don't know. Women and their feeble minds can't understand men's things such as politics."

Tamar lifted her eyebrows. She was well versed in the law, more than any attorney she knew in the states of Missouri or Kansas. *That knowledge of the law helps when you are treated like a criminal.*

"They want your neck in the loop of a noose."

Tamar shuddered at that thought. Enough women and men of the race were caught up in a lynch mob's ropes and fagots. "The issue had been put to bed. There's nothing that can be done."

"You have another letter from him in this issue."

"And I will in the next edition."

"He is very prolific in between his robberies and thieving."

Tamar smirked at the accusation. "Law-abiding men have the same opportunity to write columns. I have been waiting on your words for months."

That shut up Charles, a proud businessman who loved his craft and thought he knew things better than anyone else, but the man could not write a simple sentence to save his life. "You are my brother-in-law, and I respect and appreciate your brotherly concern." At that Charles beamed. *Men,* she realized. *It was so easy to butter them up with sweet and velvet-toned compliments.*

"Just because you consort with that man—"

Tamar spoke over his rant. "Hardly consort. I don't know him." Her answer was edged in ice and warning. This discussion about Deadwood was approaching intimate territory.

Deadwood Dick, the man who made her shiver with delight and the lover she craved to have. Not that he would ever know that. Not that they would ever be that. Men like him and women such as herself didn't share company or beds.

Yet, he made her yearn for loving, something she deserved if she was honest with her thoughts and truthful about the whispers she said in the dark. The question sparked her curiosity and burned through the safe distance she had with him.

Could I be the woman he longed for? Could he want me?

Yes, it could be her. It was her. The spinster wanted to know him carnally. Reality dashed those hopes. He was young, she was not. She was respectable, he was not. They would never meet so she could be honest with the man.

Charles snapped her back into reality. "We have night riders approaching."

Nightriders in the South meant one thing—the Kluxers—but here in this part of the country carved up before the war, nightriders only meant people riding their horses in the depth of the evening. Kansas City, still this close to the dawn of the new century, was still a paradise for men and women on the dark side of the law. She guessed that they were probably thieves, robbers, and the lawless, especially coming through this part of town. Tamar exhaled and rolled her shoulders, her hand brushing against the weapon strapped to her waist. If they were coming for trouble, she was prepared. Her shotgun and pistol were loaded and ready.

CHAPTER EIGHT

A light glowed in the offices of the *Advocate*. The only spot of light on the street. Good, church-going folks were in their beds, waiting for the cock to crow at dawn to wake them up for service. The heathens were out still, causing problems or getting between the first welcoming pair of thighs that wanted them.

Tamar was neither a sinner nor a saint, just a working woman. She was burning the midnight oil, publishing her pride and joy.

A flash of pride skittered through Amos as he watched Tamar through the window still marred by a round bullet hole, diligently stacking the newspapers into piles for delivery. He knew her hands, no matter how hard she tried to keep them clean and neat, would have ink caked on her palms and she might have a smudge on her cheek. Tamar had accomplished all of this on her own, and even with her sisters and helpers, she still did everything necessary to make this paper come alive every other week.

Amos gave a quick glance around to observe this square of land. He adjusted the handkerchief over the lower half of his face. Now he was muffled up to the eyes, and no one could see who he is. Not everyone needed to know his steps and location, especially with the heist happening so soon. One false move and everything he worked for could evaporate.

He shook those thoughts from his mind. He was here for Tamar. He tied up his horse and bounded up the steps two at a time. The door was closed, but he could hear the discussion inside.

A masculine voice spoke first. "It's too late for two single women to be out alone." Amos frowned, wondering what man would be worried about Tamar's safety. A pulse of possessiveness jarred him. She was not his, but he felt compelled to be concerned about her safety and whether the men in her life meant harm.

The other woman—Amos assumed her younger sister Delilah based on her fresh-faced enthusiasm—patted her hip. "Charles, we can handle ourselves. We have protection."

"Not including the shotgun back here. I am tempted to use it on your hide," Tamar said pointedly at Charles.

Without a knock, he tied a bandana over his lower face came into the office. The bell over the door tinkled, and Tamar, her sister and co-publisher, and the man she called Charles swiveled around to see him stroll into the office. He expected the man to recognize him, but the scarf and his hat hid most of his features. "And I am sure she knows how to use it," Amos said. "Miss Freeman, it's a pleasure to see you." He omitted the "again" he wanted to use because of the company in the room. "I hope we aren't intruding."

"We?" Tamar asked, surprised to see two other masked men appear behind him.

"Me and a few pals had business to handle. This is the last stop I needed to make."

Her eyebrows rose at the statement, a smile creasing her face. She was as tiny as he remembered, barely reaching his shoulder. She had a jawline that could cut glass and a determined glance that should shred the average man to the thinnest ribbon one could find. But here she looked sweet and innocent. The caution and causticness she gave out all day disappeared.

"I wish I could say it's a pleasure to see you in the flesh." She touched his hand to shake it, and a flash of lightning, a spark of something wild jolted through him.

Tamar jerked away as if she touched fire. Amos knew then that she felt it too. He smiled as he tipped his hat to her. "The flesh is better than the myth. Did you receive the opinion?"

She nodded. "I will run it. You have a great gift with the pen. It is a pity that you chose what you do. The pen is mightier than the sword."

Amos laughed. "But it doesn't pay that well."

"How much do you make as an outlaw?"

"Not very much for the chances I take," he said.

"Why are you here?" Charles interjected himself into the conversation.

"It's good to have a friend. It's better to see a friend."

"I'm hardly a friend to every gallant outlaw who comes into town." Tamar dropped her head so he could not see the joy on her face, but he knew it was there. She was a proud woman who had never had a man treat her to sincere compliments.

"I hope your friendship with an outlaw is just reserved for me."

Charles thumped his hand on the counter and growled at the men. "See what I am talking about? Criminals ride through town with little impunity."

"I'm not the typical criminal," said Amos, his gaze turning cold. "You speak as though you know me." He was a gentleman criminal. The rest of the gang he was riding with, he could not say the same about. They were jaded, crusty men who stole for pleasure and with impunity.

Charles released a garbled laugh. "All criminals are the same."

"I am assuming that you are—"

"I am Charles Henderson, owner of the Lincoln Barber Shops. An honest businessman. Nothing you would know about."

Amos nodded. The man had a lock on the city with his fine establishment. He wondered if Charles knew how many of the upstanding men he serviced had their hands, elbows, and entire arms sunk into the criminal element. He turned to Tamar who rolled her eyes. "What is he to you?"

Under her breath, she gave her answer. "A tick that can't be removed."

He tsked under his breath. "No need for name calling, Miss Tamar."

The familiarity of him using her Christian name shocked the room. Delilah gasped, and Charles charged toward him, shouting. "How dare you call her by her God-given name!"

Amos nodded, and the other men in black wrestled with Charles and then flipped him over so he was dangling.

"If you want him killed, we can oblige," Luke whispered. "I will bring his head to you—"

Tamar's eyes widened, and she raised her hands. "No, not necessary. He's actually a good man. I believe his head is an important part to my sister Priscilla." She looked from the black-clad men holding Charles to Amos. "Please have them stop. My sister would kill us."

The men's eyes swung to the other woman in the room. Luke eyed her and then Charles. "This man is yours?"

"Not me!" shrieked Delilah. "Our middle sister, Priscilla. And I think she would prefer a whole man to a half-dead man."

Luke pulled his bandana off his face and grinned with devilish delight. "So you are not spoken for."

"She's off-limits, cowboy," Tamar said.

"You scoundrels should not talk with her like this," Charles shouted.

"Take him outside." Amos ticked his head to the side, and the men hustled the still topsy-turvy Charles outside. They shook him until the contents of his pockets dropped and rolled onto the sidewalk.

"I will go and make sure he is okay." Delilah eyed the masked man warily. "Will you be okay?"

Tamar tapped her finger against the desk. "I will be fine. I have nothing to fear from Mr.—"

He interrupted before she slipped and called him by his real name. "My last name's not necessary. And I would not harm a hair on her head."

"It's not her hair or head that I am worried about," Delilah muttered before sprinting to the door. "She's off-limits too, cowboy."

CHAPTER NINE

Tamar gathered her skirts and swished into the back room. Amos followed, closing the door behind them. "We don't have long," she said, and he knew it was true. Too many prying eyes could see into her office.

She yawned, pressing the back of her hand to her mouth. She had to finish before her bedtime.

"Good evening, Tamar."

"Amos." She reached out to enfold her arms around him, and he backed away.

"Don't touch me. I'm dirty." He knew what he looked like: dirty denims, grubby hands, wild and bushy hair covering his face and head.

"I don't like being told what to do," Tamar said, pulling him into her embrace. The crush of her breasts and hips against him undid him. Almost.

A second longer and he would have knocked his careful plans out of the loop. She loosened her grip and stepped away, reaching out to touch his cheek. He leaned into the cradling palm of her hand. Soft, just like he remembered and imagined. The outlaw sighed. "I missed you, Tamar Ruth." He kissed her hand that she promptly snatched away.

"Tell me the truth. Are you here to cause trouble?"

"I'm an outlaw. That's part of my job."

"Did you use my paper to do that?"

That little rat-faced bastard had told her the truth. Amos exhaled slowly, counting backwards to give him time to gather his thoughts and create a new lie. "I used your paper to communicate with a friend. That's all. I promise. And you said your brother-in-law hates what you do."

"He puts doubts into my head. I never listen to them, but he said—" Amos pulled her tighter and laid his lips over hers. "When I come to see you at night, wear your hair down for me. Please." He toyed with the pins holding her hair up in a tight bun.

"I will let you take it down for me one night."

He groaned. He wanted her tonight, but he had other obligations and duties to his job and his men. "Not tonight."

"You cannot tease me like this."

"I will be back. Sooner rather than later."

"Promises, promises. Tell me anything."

"The harlot and the virtuous woman. You're a contradiction."

"You remember your Bible."

"I'm a robber, not a heathen."

"Odd since you are breaking the fourth commandment."

"Remember the Sabbath day and keep it holy?"

"You're breaking the one about stealing."

"Number seven or eight, depending on the translation. I have broken that one. But I only take from those who deserve having things taken from them."

"It's still stealing," Tamar said with a playful slap to his chest. "You don't have to check on me."

"I don't have to, but I want to."

"Your responsibility is misplaced."

"You are a friend." Amos absently stroked his chin.

Tamar fumbled with the right words. "This is new to me. I've never had a male friend before. Colleagues, yes. But I doubt any of them would have taken control the other night when—" She shivered. "Thank you for everything. And running my papers."

"You're welcome." She saw her chance and stole a kiss from him. "I'm sorry if I was forward. But I've wanted to give you that all day."

"That was a surprise, Tamar."

"I know. I've never been kissed so I'm not sure if—"

"Let's resolve that now." Amos bent over and brushed his lips against hers. "First kiss. Are you ready for your second?"

She nodded. "Second and third … " She angled her head and stretched up to meet his lips. This time the kiss wasn't quick, over in a second. They teased each other with pecks and the feeling of their mingled breaths until she sighed, parting her lips slightly and then he took full advantage.

When he stopped, he whispered, "I won't apologize for my boldness. A man soon realizes that he can't live with regret."

"A woman can't live with regret either. I will accept your offer."

"My offer?" Amos raised a dark eyebrow. "I made several offers."

Tamar felt the heat prickling all over her body. "Your offer to bed me. You have wooed me and charmed me with your words. What follows next in the course of seduction?"

"You're too methodical. You have the mind of a West Point strategist. The lovers must meet again."

"We are doing that now. The next stage is … "

He whisked her into his arms, and the hug, their closeness, was enough to tide him over for a while.

"I still owe you for that last lonely hearts ad."

"Your payment was enough. I hope Ada took the break-up well."

Amos nodded. "Maybe I can pay you back with a wedding gift for your sister. Perhaps that will smooth things over with your brother-in-law."

"No, thank you. I will decline any gift."

"You don't have to worry that I absconded with someone's tokens. I have scruples and my own money, Miss Freeman." Amos leaned onto the table and pulled her between his legs. He crossed his long legs at the ankles, locking her in place while slowing raking her over with his heated gaze. "Close your eyes. What is the first thing that springs to mind from the Montgomery Ward catalog?"

"What I want isn't in a catalog."

He groaned. "You are making this difficult."

She laughed heartily. "Your kind words are enough. I am doing my job."

He stroked her hair and pressed his nose into the tangle of hair atop her head. "I want Delilah to know that everything is in working order."

"And none of the hairs on my head have been touched," she said, her head resting on his chest. "I know how to protect myself even if you tried anything."

"Even against your mayor? Your last piece didn't take too kindly to him."

"I can handle him blindfolded and struck dumb."

"I haven't been any place where a lady doesn't like receiving gifts."

"I am certain you keep a sweetheart in every county. And you may charm them with this, but try harder with me."

"So there will be other opportunities?"

"I would be unworthy of you if I did not tell you the whole truth. Yes, of course."

"I believe you have something for me."

Tamar passed the copy of the paper to him. "Are you far from here?"

"What good would … "

"I won't reveal where you are."

"Of course you won't because I'm not going to tell you. For your own good."

"You can trust me, Amos." Tamar covered her mouth once his name crossed her lips. "Can I say it?"

He nodded. A woman hadn't said his real name in years. He had so many names he wasn't sure what his rightful name was until she sighed it into the night air. Amos. The name his mother gave him for her father, a preacher. A sinner named after a preacher. His arms reluctantly released her, and he stepped away. "Good night, Miss Freeman. Until we meet again."

"Provided you can keep your neck out of the lawman's noose, there might be a next time."

"That may be sooner rather than later."

CHAPTER TEN

"I understand you had a visitor last night."

Tamar barely acknowledged her sister Priscilla as she worked on a paper jam in the printer. "Good morning, dear middle sister. To what do we owe the privilege?

Snatching the gloves off her hands, Priscilla repeated herself. "I understand you had a visitor last night."

Tamar whistled and tossed the wrench on the floor. Where was a good repairman when she needed him? If only Amos was here … She smiled at the thought of him and then quickly wiped it off her face when she found her sister dissecting her appearance. "Both you and your husband have a knack for repetition."

Her glamorous sister stood in the middle of the room and rocked on her toes. "Actually, you had enchanting visitors of the dark outlaw variety."

Tamar looked up from the press. "I heard you the first time." Priscilla was everything she was not: short, voluptuously shaped like a double bass, a beauty that captured the hearts of men across the territory and at Oberlin College, where she studied classical languages. Men fainted over her, fawned over her, and became enraptured with her. Even if she was just a woman with the same parts that everyone else had, Priscilla possessed something. Tamar loved her dear sister, but a tinge of envy flooded through her when she saw those gazes.

Today Priscilla was wearing an emerald green dress made of the finest silk and lace from the latest boutique and seamstress in Paris. Nothing was too good for her sister who had just come back from a honeymoon tour in Europe, a gift courtesy of Charles. Tamar glanced at her own outfit, a plain navy dress that was dark enough to hide ink smudges and paper dust. Even if she fully concentrated on every action, she could never get away with a dress like that. Her sister earned her name "Prissy" by wearing clothes that no working woman ever could manage.

Tamar ran the back of her hand over her hair, waiting for her middle sister to comment about its state and asking to put one of those new Annie Malone hair concoctions through it to make it manageable. "Who told you?"

Priscilla unfolded a sheet and spread it atop the sole chair in the office before sitting down. "You didn't answer, and you know I hate being ignored." She scanned the space that tripled as an office, print room, and packing center. "Delilah told me. Speaking of which, where is she?"

Tamar snagged the awry piece of paper and waved it victoriously. She won against the ornery machine. She threaded the sheet through the printer again and restarted the press. "Delilah is covering at the school until the new crop of teachers arrive from Howard and Oberlin. And my visitors are my business."

"Dear sister, this paper is the family business, so I have a thirty-three percent stake in whatever happens here."

Tamar rolled her eyes so hard she was surprised when they didn't stick in that position. "Charles was pillow talking, I assume. Then you know who visited me."

"Charles is huffing and puffing. He believed that we should have taken them to the authorities."

"I am sure he did." Tamar stopped, recalling what her sister said. "We?" she asked, swiveling around the press so she could see her sister face-to-face.

"Charles is the man of the family now."

"Correction, dear sister. He is the head of your household, not mine."

"Since you are unwed—"

"I was taking care of the family's affairs ever since we came here after the war to live with our grandfather. We didn't need a man then."

"You may not need a man, sister. But I do," said Priscilla, leaning on the armchair and watching Tamar. "I like having Charles around. He's only looking out for you."

Tamar sighed. "I appreciate his efforts, but I can work a shotgun, press, and balance sheet better than he can."

"I won't tell him that," Priscilla said, chuckling. Truth was all the Freeman girls could do most things better than men. That's what happened when you were raised as boys. "So the gang is back in town."

Tamar lifted her shoulders in a shrug. "I believe they are."

"You know every move Deadwood Dick makes. If I didn't know better, I would assume you are in cahoots with him."

Tamar laughed. "Could I pull off capers wearing this?"

"How do you know him?"

"I don't know him." She hated lying to her sister, but some pieces of her life she kept only for her eyes. "We know each other through letters to the paper." And how she loved getting those letters from him. The scrawl was familiar masculine handwriting she knew and loved.

"Be careful, sister."

Her state of mind had been wrapped up in other concerns and issues. "I will. I'm used to taking care of myself."

"You should consider Mr. Marshall as a life partner."

Tamar rolled her eyes at the mention of the old banker who had been keen on her for years. "Not that again. I'm not marrying him or anyone else."

Priscilla wagged her finger. "He's a good man," she countered.

A good and ancient man, Tamar thought. The man in question was closer in age to Methuselah than to her. He was old when she first met him, and he had not visited the Fountain of Youth since that time. "I have no argument about his goodness. But a marriage cannot be sustained with just goodness."

"You should have passion."

Tamar shook her head. Passion was something that she'd never had. Tamar didn't realize how much she missed as a woman until her night trapped with Amos. *Heck, the only kiss I ever got was fabulous. Was it like this for every woman?* Heat rushed through her as she remembered the vivid experience of that night. She felt so alive. Her senses were sharpened; even now in the light of the day and in the middle of this trifling conversation, she could feel the intimate caress of his fingers and mouth against her neck, the push of his body against hers, being sandwiched between the wall and his firm body, the hardness that … Her mind was racing to places she could not go. She still had a business to run and editorials to publish. She directed her attention back to Priscilla's mouth and caught her in mid-monologue.

" … it's such a shame to never experience intimate and intense passion, Tamar."

"It is," she murmured. "But it is not meant to be. Some women are not built for that."

"Don't you get lonely?"

"I have my noble work," Tamar said, patting the press lovingly. "And a cranky press. But I love what I do."

"But the paper can't hold you at night."

"I like sleeping alone."

"I don't. There's nothing like—" Priscilla blushed and beckoned her sister closer. "There is a lot of joy to be had in bed with a man," she said in a hushed whisper.

Tamar almost gagged but smiled weakly instead. She tried to bar the images of her sister and her portly, beloved husband doing anything in bed besides sleeping. "You're a married woman. You should take pleasure in the marital bed."

"I had pleasure before marriage. I want the same for you, even if you are beyond prime marriage years. I'm with a baby, and I want the same kind of happiness for you I am feeling," Priscilla said, trapping her sister's hand in her own.

Tamar turned to face the wall. She never felt that bubble of happiness about becoming a mother, and given her age she probably never would. "If there is anything I can do … "

"Sister, we would like the house. That old house is too big for you."

"It's my house. Our house. It belongs to the family."

"And a family should be inside of it. Just give it a thought, please, sister." Priscilla dropped her sister's hand and started to the door. "And stop entertaining outlaws."

"Who is older, Priscilla?"

"You are, but that does mean you are wiser."

"Wise and wizened, Prissy. I'm not falling for an outlaw."

"You seem enamored."

"I am intrigued by the man and his story. He writes eloquently."

"He may have stolen those thoughts from someone else. I would not put it past him."

"The words he writes are his own. He's incredibly intelligent and thoughtful. If you met him—"

"You met him before last night."

"And if I have?" Tamar asked.

"You need to be cautious. He is a criminal."

"He is a gentleman."

"Gentlemen do not steal or take advantage of bluestockings. I swear you are losing your mind."

"Worry about your baby and your husband, Priscilla."

"Tell me you won't see him again. Promise me, sister." Priscilla extended her pinky finger, the traditional way the sisters made agreements.

Tamar grasped her sister's pinkie finger with her own. "I doubt I will see him again. Promise on my printing press."

Priscilla nodded, her lips pursed and her eyes narrowed. "I know you crave passion and trouble underneath your political rabble-rousing nonsense. Just not with that man. He will hurt you."

Tamar pulled her pinkie finger out of the grip and gave an impatient shrug. "Don't believe my word. But know that no man can hurt me or make me do anything I don't want to do."

"When you fall in love, you will do things for your man that you never imagined. Just don't fall for him," Priscilla said, her voice an octave lower. "Give me your word."

"You should go home, Priscilla." Tamar smiled and inclined her head to the office's main door. "I can take care of myself." Once she watched her sister flounce out of the office, Tamar opened the latest stack of mail, certain that she would experience pleasure with him.

"Are you okay?" Delilah touched her sister's back. "I think you're crying."

Tamar stuffed down the last sets of tears and whimpers. "My eyes are tired. I think I need a break. Can you handle—"

Delilah nodded. "Sure, take care of yourself. It's that outlaw, isn't it?"

Tamar shook her head as she fastened a bonnet around her head. "Never trust a bad man, Delilah. It's not worth it."

CHAPTER ELEVEN

Across town in the boardinghouse with thin walls, decrepit furniture, and suspect tenants, Amos laid down and thought about the job he had to do. The men he had to betray.

"Damn it," Amos whispered, the curse bouncing off the walls. He was sick of this life. Tired of the conditions. Ready for his double life between outlaws and Pinkertons to be complete. He served his time with valor and now he wanted peace.

When he'd had the small sliver of peace on his farm and patrolling the Indian Country, he'd wanted more. Craved excitement.

But now he'd had enough.

It was enough to drive a man to drink.

Amos headed to the closest open saloon he could find and once there the darkest corner that the long oak bar led him to.

A glass of whisky later, he was temporarily warmed and sated. The drink did its job.

"Another?" The working girl stopped by his table with a friendly smile and offering anything he could want—drink, drugs, two women willing to do whatever you asked them to do.

He wanted conversation. Amos pulled the seat out and laid a bill on the table. "Sit down."

She obeyed, eyeing the bill. "It's yours," he said, watching her tuck it into her bosom. "What's your name?"

"Kitty."

"Your real name."

"Lucy Pearl." A hint of Mississippi slipped out with her real name.

"You been here long?"

"A few months. It's good money."

Amos shook his head. "No it's not. Go home."

"Can't go home. There's nothing there."

"This place will eat you alive. Now, where's the poker table?"

She pointed to a room past the bar, and he collected the bottle and his glass. An empty seat waited for him.

"We're playing poker, boy."

He bristled at the term the man threw at him. No one called him boy, but Amos never showed anger at the poker table. "Deal me in."

The cards slid across the table and he waited until the dealer was done to examine his hand. He lifted up the cards and cursed.

A dead man's hand, a hand full of three jacks and a pair of tens. An omen.

He took another drink and played the hand.

He won. A dead man winning, he thought gathering the pile on the table.

He left the table after another hand and headed into the larger room.

The boisterous noise of the saloon dimmed. He looked up and two women were squaring off at the center of the saloon.

"He's mine."

The sheriff stood up in the back of the room and bellowed. "Ladies, ladies, there's no need to fight and rabble-rouse like men." The woman in the red used that disruption to her advantage and struck first, felling the woman in the green.

Screams erupted. Shots fired. People fled.

Amos grabbed the bargirl and shoved a wad of bills in her hand. "Go away from here. This is not for you."

It took one to know one. He hoped she took his advice. Hell, he wasn't taking his own advice.

Soon he would be away from here.

But right now he was stuck in this city, trapped in this life.

He needed healing. He needed an escape.

He needed Tamar.

Tonight was perfect. The full moon illuminated the streets that had yet to be given the artificial lights that beamed and shone through downtown. He peered around in the darkness for any other souls wandering the streets. He waited in the night's shadows across the street from the *Advocate's* offices. The boarded-up windows hid the activity from the rest of the world, but he knew she was still in there. Bart kept his promise to her, and the man assigned to watch her business waited at the door until she was ready to leave for the evening.

More like the morning, he thought. It was minutes past midnight, and sleep was about to overtake the man nodding on his post. A rookie mistake if Amos ever saw one. An agent never sleeps.

He had no reason to be here tonight. Something about her pulled him back here. He wanted to make sure she was doing well, possibly give her some delight if she was down. She had been attacked, and all he wanted to do was comfort her and make sure she was safe and protected.

And he wanted to feel her kisses again. "Let me not lie," he muttered. He wanted to know her in the most carnal way possible. He wanted to lie with her, pull her into the curve of his body and wake up with a sweet smelling woman beside him. Or on top of him. He wanted to spend some real time with her, spoil her.

But all they could have were these stolen moments in the dark.

He watched the man walk her home to the two-story, gabled-front residence where she lived. Amos knew she would enter through the front door, secure that entrance, and then head to the back porch that overlooked a riotous wedge of flowers and grass. He waited for the man to disappear before he slid into the darkness and into her backyard. He crept along the shadows of the street and homes. Cautious, even now. His neck to the average man was worth a lot. Bringing him in dead or alive could fetch a man a handsome sum. Sure, it would wreck an undercover operation, but no one knew that. Tonight was a risky proposition, but one he had to take.

"I see you," she said, raising her lamp to cut through the darkness. "Good morning."

He held a finger to his lips and pointed upward to the window overlooking the garden. "You'll wake your sister."

"Delilah sleeps like a rock. You're beginning to form a habit of coming to visit me."

"I wanted to make sure all was well with you. That's all."

"Is that the only reason you're here?"

He shook his head. "No, not at all. I want to tell you my story."

"Is there anything else?"

"If I may be so forward, I want to lie with you and know you, Tamar." Tonight. Forever. This time, the air was thick with desire, choking both of them with anticipation and expectation. Unlike the last time he did this, there was no mistrust or uncertainty on their parts. They had dropped mythical selves—the thief, the feared journalist—and were just a man and woman who finally fell to the slow, intense throb of attraction.

"Come with me." She beckoned for him to follow her up the stairs and into the house. Amos felt as though he knew the interiors of this house, knowing which boards squeaked and the placement of the rooms. If it were daylight and he'd had the audacity to enter through the front, he'd see the large fireplace and her treasured library. She hooked through the maze of hallways and arrived into a study lined with books and heavy furniture.

"This is my study." She blew on the lamp in her hand and then extinguished the lamp lighting the room. The only light beaming into the room was the full moon through the slits in the curtains.

She pressed two fingers to his lips. All this time, aching for his kiss and touch. That single moment almost undid her. A soft moan escaped her lips. He was going to go slow tonight, have a good and innocent moment with her.

Her moan and the light in her eyes ground his best intentions into dust. He kissed her. A soft touch just to appease the tingling beast of arousal in him. But he wanted more.

"I brought a gift."

She pried the box lid open. "Taste it. Sweets for the sweet."

"I've never had— What do you call these?" she asked, dropping one on her tongue.

"Pralines." He plucked one from the box. "It's like heaven in your mouth."

"Do you ever wonder about the lives of the people you take from?"

"I don't. This is business." He put the box on the table. "You keep those. I know that you enjoyed them."

Her fingers traced the embellishment on the box, avoiding his eyes. "Maybe these were meant for someone's child or beloved."

"Or maybe he was a fat man who was going to gorge on them at home."

Tamar shook her head. "You should stop this. I'm a publisher."

"You're still a lady. I haven't been any place where a lady doesn't like receiving gifts."

"And you may charm them with this, but try harder with me."

Amos nodded, sucking the sugar off his fingers. "I will study your every wish if you will give me the right to do so."

She watched him with smug delight. "I only have one request. I want your story. How did you, a sweet, preacher's son, become a villain?"

He leaned back into the chair, his mouth tight and grim. "Until I met you, I wasn't interested in telling my story to anyone except maybe my children."

"You have—" Confusion crossed her face. "A family already?"

Amos shook his head. "No. When I do, I will tell them all my exploits. Strictly as fiction, not as a to-do manual."

"Are you married?"

"Nothing of the sort. It was never right."

Tamar nodded. "I understand. I was engaged once, but he died. This newspaper was one of his favorite causes, and I threw myself into it because of him, to honor his memory."

He kissed her forehead. "My sweet lady. You've done a wonderful job. I ended up here because I needed the money. I didn't need a lot but when it started coming, I couldn't stop."

"What will make you stop? The law or the commandments haven't worked." *Maybe the love of a good woman.*

He shifted uncomfortably. "When it's time, I will quit."

"And is it time? I'm sorry but I'm curious. I have a thousand questions for everyone."

"Ask them. I am willing to tell you what you want to know." He punctuated his statement with a kiss.

"I lose my words when I am around you."

"Close your eyes. Pretend that I am not here."

"What do you want from me? I'm not a rich woman. I'm not—"

"You're beautiful. You're desirable. You are more than I could ever have in this life." Amos stopped, looking out of the window.

She gulped, avoiding his thoughtful, absorbing gaze. He took everything in about his environment, reading the room and trusting his intuition. Her eyes, he thought, would tell him everything. Her body told him the entire story. "I don't like you being here. I've had thoughts about you. Impure, untoward thoughts that an old maid should not have."

"You are hardly old."

"But I am a maiden. I've never been with a man."

"Does that terrify you? The idea of lying with a man?"

"Never. I just never wanted to do that before I met you. You make me covet things I don't have. And I feel funny like you've lit a match to a sparkler inside of me. It feels like gas but different."

Amos laughed a full-bodied chuckle that prompted her to smother his mouth with her hand. "That was the most romantic thing you've probably ever said. But that's what desire feels like, except the gas part."

"I do not wish to desire you. There must be a tonic I can take to cleanse myself of this."

"Nothing can cure you of that. You can't get rid of it quickly."

"You're saying that because you want me to succumb to your charms."

"I cannot seduce a woman who doesn't want to be."

"Men here aren't like you. You say these words as if they are true."

"I wouldn't say them if they weren't true."

"To me? Kansas City men think I'm Medusa. Have I turned you into stone?" She raised his large right hand against her own, and he was absorbed in the contrasts: hard and calloused, soft and smooth, large to small. She clutched his hand and raised the palm to her mouth, planting a kiss. Her gaze matched his. "I want the story of your scars. Show them all to me, please."

"You just want my stories." He withdrew his hand and stepped away from her and toward the study's door. "Sleep on it. It may go away later. I have to leave."

"I want you, Amos. All of you, stories, scars, and stone, now. Please let me at least see them."

• • •

He pulled off his coat and the outer layers until all she saw was his chest. His tall, lean frame betrayed the solid muscles that rippled with his movements. Fine black hair covered his forearms and swirls of that same black hair covered his— Tamar swallowed for the correct words. "Pectoral muscles," she blurted, remembering the words her sister Delilah used when studying anatomy from a used, battered medical book.

"Excuse me," he said, stopping to face her. She stepped backward, and the corner of the roll top desk jabbed her in the back. She mewled in pain, and he moved toward her. His hand connected with her hip and lower back before she could say anything. Excitement and anticipation threaded through her body. She felt warm and dizzy, excited and animated, restless and on edge. It was as if fire had shot through her bones and was melting her from the inside out.

It was him. His touch. His presence. Just the masculine energy that was bouncing in this space that normally had none. His hand slipped lower right above her bottom and massaged the spot she hit. "That must have hurt," he muttered, concentrating on his slight massage and not her face. If she could blush, she would be as crimson as a rose. If she was a loose woman she— Tamar sighed. She had no idea what she would have done. Men never came to her with the ease her sister Priscilla had.

Until tonight. At least she had felt a man's touch beyond a gentle hand to help her out of carriage and a slight brush of hands when passing the beans at a dinner table. Those polite gestures never consumed her or provoked her lust. Only Amos did that to her.

She broke free and stepped away from him. The more distance and objects she could put between them, the better for her sanity. A jolt of that unusual feeling played hide-and-go-seek between her legs, and she liked it more than a good, upstanding spinster should. She shook her head out of those thoughts and focused on him again.

He was still undressing. Have mercy. The marbling and marring of his perfect skin by bullets and other wounds. Tamar wanted to touch them and curl up with him as he told her his stories for each bullet dodged and lodged. She cleared her throat, trying to find her voice. "Every man doesn't have stories to tell with each scar, but I am certain you do."

Her eyes widened as the man continued to disrobe. His hands fiddled with the closure of his dungarees as he kicked off his boots. She closed her eyes, unsure if she was supposed to continue staring at this striptease.

"Open your eyes, ma'am," he said.

She popped open her lids, and she shook her head at the sight. He was naked as a jaybird, his hands barely concealing his privates. Her eyes roamed over his perfect form. Such a thing like this belonged in a great museum. He was all planes, contours, and muscles. Not an ounce of fat on him. He was perfect like that statue she once saw in a painting. The Michelangelo. Except he was much bigger down there, she thought, slowly pulling her eyes away from the limp cock hanging between his thighs.

"This still doesn't tell you anything," he said. "I know that. But I'm a man, bare as the day he is born. I have no weapon or ulterior motives. Just desire for you."

She reached out and touched the clump of scarred skin tissue on his left shoulder. "What happened—"

He swallowed when her cool fingers traced his warm skin, learning the topography of the injury—the peaks and valleys of his body, the mottled places where someone tried to kill him. Just touching him created a sizzle of excitement stretching from the pads of her fingers to the roots of her coiled hair. A flash of leapt into her and spread across her skin. She wanted to be engulfed by his touch. Whatever she felt, she wanted more of it and soon. She kissed the scar. Under his lips, she shuddered with a sagging breath. The blaze burning inside melted him.] She guided him to the wall of the study as she continued her exploration.

"This one," she asked, trailing her finger across his collarbone to his throat. "Who did this?"

"A man in Texas. Do you conduct every interview like this?"

She laughed, a deep octave rimmed with an emotion she never felt. Hunger, eagerness, craving. She put a pin in that thought and decoded what she felt. "*For God's sake, hold your tongue and let me love*," she said, using his own words against him.

His checkered past was displayed all over his body. The last wound was above his hip. She fell to her knees, her skirts fanning around her. The evidence of his arousal intrigued her, and she reached between them to caress the length of him.

"If you keep that up, I'm going to spend in your hand."

She released him reluctantly, only to slip his member into her mouth eagerly, with a guarded boldness.

"I cannot handle your mouth there. Please stop."

"What are you feeling?"

"I want to explode. I'm weak but feel like I could take on 10,000 men. Don't—"

She rose to her feet and slid a hand over his hard cock while the other snaked around his neck. He pressed forward so their mouths collided. His moan of release and pleasure filled her mouth as he overflowed into her hand. She continued to pump and kiss, kiss and pump until he had nothing else to give.

"Now, it's my turn. Tell me the story of your scars, Tamar."

"Come," she said. Her boldness shocked her. She grabbed the hem of her nightgown and lifted it off her body, tossing it carelessly to the ground.

He ran his hands down the curve of her back until he cupped her full bottom. With his free hand, Amos unwound the mass of hair atop of her head and she shook out the curls, letting the waves of hair cascade down her shoulders and breasts and down her back. They were like Adam and Eve, nude in their own secret garden.

"So beautiful." He easily picked her up and laid her across the pallet of blankets on the wooden floor. His gaze stole over her, tracing every line and curve of her body. His hands followed the path, stroking the sides of her cheeks.

He palmed her breasts, a thumb flicking over the tip of her nipples. A shot of pleasure coursed through her body in response. She bit her lip. "Tamar, am I hurting you?"

"No. Don't hold back."

He grinned as he plucked one nipple into his mouth. He laved the diamond hard tip and drew back to blow. Before she could complain, his mouth was back on her, sucking, tugging and pulling. One hand wrapped around her waist, drawing her closer and the other pinched the other nipple.

He was the spark to her kindling. Heat pooled in her brain and between her legs.

"I've waited so long for this night," she said, mumbling her words. She was drunk off the nearness of him.

"Open for me, Tamar," he said, a slurred murmur against her lips before he tasted her tongue again. He slipped lower, kissing his way down her body. Tamar thought he would stop, but he ventured lower. A man shouldn't—

All the thoughts evaporated from her head when his fingers tapped on the lips hidden in a nest of dark curls. The thrill vibrated across her body and she arched and opened for him.

"You're beautiful," he whispered. Tamar laughed, raising a fist to cut off her chuckle. He rewarded her by settling between her thighs and stealing the pillow, contorting the fluffy mass into a wedge-like shape, and stuffing it under her hips. "If I cannot convince you with my words, let me convince you in other ways. A bashful woman would have been shocked by this," Amos said.

Tamar relished at the angle and the sight before her. The man she enjoyed and loved was worshipping her, lapping at the pearl and kissing her nether lips with abandon. Yes, a bashful lady would be shocked, but the brazen woman, finally blossoming through the sensuous pleasures Amos introduced to her, wanted more. This felt so good and so right.

She came, a cocoon of delight and pleasure swaddling her body. He pressed the head of his cock into her. The man was an expert in slow torture. He took his time, pressing into her and filling her up only to retreat. His strokes were measured, languorous, and spiraling her into madness.

"Give me your delight," she whispered. He silenced her by circling her button as he stroked. Tamar couldn't form complete thoughts, and the words flew out of her head. "Now." The command prodded him to move faster. He leaned down, scooping in to wrap her legs around his body and steal a kiss from her. She milked him with each fast stroke. At her edge, she locked eyes with him. He tumbled soon after. He collapsed on top of her. His weight wasn't unbearable; rather his skin on her skin was a comfort.

CHAPTER TWELVE

Amos snatched his pocket watch off the stand and peered at the Arabic numerals, computing the time in his head. Four in the morning on the day of his reckoning. He laid the watch back on the table and stared at the ceiling; the warm feminine body next to him searched him out. Her fingers sliding across the pillows until she made contact with flesh. She curled into him, her legs twining with his. This was natural, this was real. This could never happen again. Not like this, not with him still in character.

Amos turned his head and watched Tamar sleep. Knowing that she was shy about her body, he dressed her] once they finished making love. The shift stretched over the swell of her stomach. She moved, kicking the covers off her legs, exposing the thatch of black hair at the apex of her thighs. He wished he could still be inside of her sweetness or have the taste of her on his tongue again.

He resisted. The time had come. He needed to leave her and this life behind. He leaned down and pecked her on the forehead before rising to his feet.

"It's early," she whispered.

"Dawn is coming. How would it look for the scoundrel Deadwood Dick to be climbing out of your window?"

"I don't care what anyone thinks."

She may not have cared, but he did. She was a respectable woman who didn't need any tinge of grime on her reputation.

"I love you, Amos."

He stifled the urge to say, "I love you" to her. The feeling she brought out of him was confusing. "Have you said those words to anyone else?"

She turned away from him. "This is hardly the line of questioning you ask."

"You should love the man if you tell him that," Amos said, tilting her face back to his face.

Tamar frowned, tracing the seams of the blanket with her eyes and fingers. "You should stop stealing."

"True. I should. There are a lot of shoulds we have in our lives, but I haven't found the right reason to stop. Until now," he said with a soft kiss to her lips.

Tamar could hardly enjoy the kiss. "Me?" she asked, breaking apart and tilting his chin so she could look in his eyes. "I'm the one that is going to make you go on the straight and narrow."

"If I could be a good man, I would for you." His eyes darkened as he held her gaze. "You deserve better than me."

"But I want you." Tamar let out a long, audible breath. "I feel different when I'm with you. Cherished. Beloved. You discard the shell of me and see me as how I am."

He gathered her into him and settled her on top of him. He was amazed at how easily they fit together, how effortlessly it took for both of them to become aroused. Shyly, she pulled her hair and her hands over her breasts. "Don't hide from me, Tamar," he said, brushing aside her hands and kissing her nipples into hardened peaks.

"I'm not hiding. I have never been with a man like this. It's awkward."

He still had some things to teach her in the small window of time they had. Wordlessly, he propped himself up with the pillows, still anchoring her to him with his hands firm on her hips. He lifted her a fraction to slide his member into her. A moan escaped her lips as she sank onto him and her hips undulated.

Nature took over. She rode him precisely up and down. He watched her wetness coat his cock, her cunny taking as much of him as she could. She controlled the tempo and intensity. She took his lips. His hips rode up to meet her pumps. Her fingers slipped to touch her aching nipples. He responded by taking one into his mouth, and his fingers took her queen, her clitty.

Spent, she leaned onto his chest, still slowly winding her hips and tightening her muscles around his cock. She was milking him and slowly killing him. He came in a quick burst inside of her and she came soon after.

Sheen of perspiration covered her, turning her skin bronze. His bronze goddess. She was his now, and he was hers forever. He smiled at that.

She tapped the corners of his mouth. "What's the smile for?"

He answered with a quick peck to her lips. "This night."

"It's now morning. You have to go."

He had to leave. Otherwise he couldn't let his mind stray. He had a mission to fulfill. His last one before he vanished.

I love you, Tamar Ruth. "I have to go," he echoed.

He rose from the floor and pulled on his clothes. He kept his back to her so he wouldn't have to see her pain and longing. He felt the same.

"When will I see you again?" She spoke first.

She wanted more time with him. But did she want the man or the outlaw?

"It's not safe for you right now. I will let you know when the time is right."

"How will you get a message to me?"

"I will find a way regardless of where I am." Amos reached into his bag and pulled out a cigar box. He laid it between them. "That's for you."

Tamar pried open the box and gasped. There were stacks of money and coins. A letter and train ticket were at the bottom. "Where did this come from?"

Amos smiled, cupping her face with his large hand, his eyes looking directly at her. "I do have my own dinero. Earned and legitimate money. I have a working ranch."

"Where?"

"South of here. Between the Canadian and Arkansas Rivers, where orderly chaos reigns."

Tamar nodded, her eyes dropping and her fingers toying with the frayed threads of the quilt. He was talking about the Canadian District, the piece of Cherokee territory between those two rivers. He wanted to tell her about the land.

She cut through the silence. "You are full of contradictions. An outlaw with land. A man who cherishes sweets and me." She raised his hands to her lips and brushed kisses on his knuckles and fingertips. "Who is the real man here?"

"If anything should ever happen to me, go there."

"Are you expecting something should happen to you?"

Amos lifted his broad shoulders in a shrug. "No man knows the day or time of his death." He did. He knew, but wasn't able to tell her. He twisted the plain band off his finger and slid it onto her thumb, the only place where it would fit. "Set me as a seal upon thine heart, for love *is* strong as death."

She twisted the ring on her finger. Tears wet her cheeks, gathering on her lashes. Have mercy. The tears of a woman he loved could undo a man. "Song of Songs?"

"You're right."

"This isn't the end, Amos. Is it?"

He kissed her forehead. *I hope not.* He couldn't tell her that. "Never. We will see each other again."

CHAPTER THIRTEEN

Dead men tell no tales, and Deadwood Dick was a walking dead man.

He faced the blue wash of sky before him. With each day he was closer to her and closer to his fate.

His fate was secured by the noose some wanted around his neck, the man hunting his crew for society's good, and the bounty on his head.

By this time next week, Deadwood Dick would be dead, and Amos Tanner would be reborn.

No one in this world would notice the difference except for two people. One of them was on his tail, shadowing his movements. The man he left behind in Kansas City, holding his money and secrets. The other was the woman who had fallen for him, the woman who knew his name but didn't know *him*.

"Let's mount up," he said, swinging his horse toward the city.

One of Amos's henchmen rode up beside him. Luke was a bad man who made his name with all the thieveries and killing he had done for years across the territories. Amos's blood boiled with every interaction with this man, but he was part of the plan. If Luke happened to die that day as well, Amos hoped it was the pine-box, six-feet-deep death.

Luke spoke first. "Plan is still the same, boss?"

He nodded. He was leading these men to danger and maybe their own deaths. They trusted him, thought he was just like them. If only they knew the truth, that he wore a tin star and was double crossing them ... He shook his head. Their day of reckoning would come, and he would pay the price for the sins of the past five years.

There's a season for everything, the Good Book said. This season was ending. He didn't want to lose the one beautiful thing that had blossomed from this deception. He would lose her before he could have her. If he were smart, he would leave this alone.

He was a smart man most hours of the day. But he was a dumb man closer to having his real life back. A life where he could make her his, legally and romantically. Dumb or smart, he was a man in love, and love made a man stupid, eager, foolish.

• • •

Amos led them to the promised land of milk and honey. The last train of the day. The train carried no passengers when it reached the depot but it did hold a wealth of bills and coins being shipped between banks. Few men dared to rob the locomotives but when they did dare they walked away with a lot of money.

Only he knew that no one was walking out of this situation and into freedom.

The train depot looked deserted in the light of the early morning. But weeks of scoping out the station and the route let them know otherwise.

Two men were in the back of the depot, leaving Amos and Luke up on the bluff, awaiting a safe getaway. They watched the men make their progress to the building. The tallest one—Frank White, one of the meanest drunks and robbers you could ever find—slipped his mask up higher on his face and strode through the doors. Through the windows, they watched them raise their guns and saw the men inside comply.

Coins and paper bills were stacked and stuffed into bags. They were almost done. Amos counted. The men were to have the money in their hands before they walked out of the door and into the awaiting nest of Pinkertons.

"What the hell—" Luke muttered. The remainder of his words were cut off by yelling and ringing shots. Both men—the lawman turned criminal and the true criminal—turned their faces and guns toward the front of the depot.

Amos swung his head and saw all the Pinkertons swarm outside of the entrances. Dammit, the team was early. Too early.

They watched as the lawmen took over the building.

"It's over," Luke said, drawing up to his full height from the crouched position. "They got them. They sure as hell aren't getting us. I'm going south. We'll meet up in Dodge City to regroup."

"The hell we will," Amos said, spitting out his words. He stalked to Luke and reached him before he got onto his horse. He threw the slight man to the ground. "It's over. You're going to jail and face the years you've earned."

"This is a setup."

"*Was* a setup," Amos said. "Get up and take your punishment like a man." He found the rope he'd stashed for this occasion in his saddlebag.

"I told them not to trust you," Luke mumbled. "You were too good to be true. No copper would do the things you did."

"I am a sheriff and a Pinkerton agent."

"No real copper would," Luke said, hate piercing his words. "You're as guilty as the rest of us. I should put a bullet through your skull."

"For what? Obeying my orders?"

"You're a liar and thief. They aren't taking me alive. And they ain't taking you until you're in a grave."

A disembodied voice rang out from below. "Tanner! Tanner!"

Distracted, Amos turned his head to his boss. "I'm fine. Dealing with this one up here. I need cover."

His boss gave a thumbs-up and moved to the huddle of agents. When Amos refocused, Luke jammed his head into his chin. Stunned, he stepped back and loosened his grip on Luke.

The prisoner made a dash for his horse. "Stop!" Amos shouted. The prisoner stopped, and slowly turned. The smile on his lips and the pistol in his hand told him that the crazed man was going to use it. "Don't point a gun unless you are going to use it," he said, patting his side.

"Your gun, Amos. All those years of pickpocketing comes in handy. Turn around."

Amos growled and flared his nostrils. "You would shoot a man in his back, coward. You would shoot an unarmed man."

"Damn right. You sold us out." Luke chuckled. "Prison is one hell I don't want to experience again. I never should have trusted you."

True, Amos thought. "Shoot me and you will die like the other two down there."

"Death will be sweeter than living in a cell. I'm prepared for that. I don't get on my knees for any man. I won't die like a coward, but you will."

Shots rang out in the dark. Too close for comfort. Bullets were coming and going. One skirted him. Another hit, tearing through the flesh, bone, and sinew of his abdomen. Instinct girded his hand up to the wound. Pulling it back he saw the blood covering his hand. All these years he had been saved. Now he knew he was a dead man. He closed his eyes and prayed, wished and hoped as the breath wheezed out of his body. He was going and his last promise to her would never be fulfilled. He was going to expire here. Alone. In the dark. It was hardly the life he'd imagined or the end he'd thought about.

"He's over here! And find that son of a bitch Luke. He's going to pay hell for this." He heard the voice. His eyes fluttered open to see Bart looming over him.

The faces changed to colors dancing before his eyes.

Life was leaving his body with each painful breath. Death is hardly pretty. And then every noise dimmed. He slipped out of consciousness, with Tamar as his last remembered thought.

CHAPTER FOURTEEN

He didn't come back the next night.

Or the night after.

Or the night following that.

After the lonesome nights, she stopped counting the days that had passed since they'd made reckless love in her study. She stopped going into that room, and although she fought it, the memory of that night receded. She longed for his touch and his kisses, and nothing could sate her. The edge of spring passed into the thick of the summer, and the answer never came. The notice never arrived. It had been weeks since she'd heard from him, but Tamar clung to hope and the words he'd whispered to her. Her heart was full of belief that this love could come true and continually warred with her mind that began to doubt.

As the season shifted, she grew cantankerous and restless. Her clothes didn't fit correctly. She felt odd cravings. She was easily winded and irritated.

Today was no different. She spent her morning fussing at Old Bertha, shooing Charles out of her hair and office, and wrote a small yet scalding opinion piece. The bell above the door rang, and she looked up to see Priscilla.

"Good afternoon, lovelies," her sister said as she strolled into the office. Delilah said hello back, but all Tamar could do was grunt.

"How long has she been like this?" Priscilla asked in a whisper loud enough for all ears to hear.

"She was unpleasant to Charles again," Delilah answered, shuffling some papers.

Priscilla giggled. "That's not unusual. It would be unusual if she hadn't barked at him today."

"This time, she cursed him." Delilah repeated the blue streak of words Tamar used.

Priscilla's eyes widened, and she pressed her handkerchief to her mouth as if the words came off her own tongue. "What's the cause of this?"

Tamar could not bear this sisterly gossiping about her anymore. "I can hear the both of you," she said, looking up from the stack of advertisements and snarling at Delilah and Priscilla. "Unless your chatter is helping to print the paper, cease with this foolish talk. I'm the same as I was before."

"You have a habit of protesting too much."

Tamar slammed the papers onto the table and rested her hands next to the pile. "I do not."

Priscilla's eyes darted down and held. Tamar followed her sister's gaze and quickly twisted the band off her finger and into a spare pocket.

Priscilla caught and pulled her hand out of the pocket. "No, don't hide that. I want to see it."

"It isn't anything, Priscilla. Don't you have some knitting to do or something? Whatever you ladies of leisure do." Tamar snatched her hand out of Priscilla's grip and waved her away. "Go and annoy your husband."

A hearty chortle exploded from Delilah and Priscilla. "You can't get rid of me that easy," her prissy middle sister said, chasing her sister around the desk. Catching up with her, she grabbed the apron and stuck her hand deep inside. "You are going to get ink all over—"

"I am washable." Priscilla withdrew the ring and held it in the sunlight beaming through the windows. "Aha! Explain this, miss."

"It's a ring," Tamar said, moving to grab it from Priscilla's grip.

"Short Stack, you can't get that from her," Delilah said with a laugh. "You need a step stool."

Priscilla huffed as she continued her examination of the ring. "You have jewelry that I have given you but refuse to wear. You haven't worn a ring on any finger ever."

Priscilla sometimes forgot the tartness of her own tongue, but Tamar forgave her. "It is a gift from a friend," she whispered, dropping her eyes and shifting her gaze to the floor, the desk, her chair, Old Bertha—anywhere but her sisters' surprised faces.

Delilah spoke first. "I'm befuddled. You don't have friends."

Priscilla shushed her younger sister. "Yes, she does. Is it the same friend who visited you—"

Tamar clamped her lips and continued to file the responses to the classified advertisements the *Advocate* ran.

"Sister, I tell you everything, and you are keeping me in the dark about this man."

"It was nothing." *It was everything.* Tamar hated to deny.

"Nothing doesn't come with a ring. Tell me, Tamar."

"He was with me, and it was pleasant."

Priscilla wrinkled her nose. "Did you use the French letter?" At her sister's puzzled response, she searched for another term. "A sheath? Or did he withdraw?"

Tamar bit the inside of her cheek. "Neither."

Priscilla clucked her tongue. Delilah's eyes narrowed to mere slits. Tamar could hear the whirring of the minds.

"You're wrong."

They both spoke at once. "You may be with—"

Tamar shook her head as she crossed her hands over her stomach. "I'm too old to have a child." She could count the number of thirty-seven-year-old women carrying babies on two hands, but all of them had a passel of little ones running about. "I'm positive," Tamar said, shaking her head. "I am not with a child."

"And if you're wrong, Tamar are you prepared for that?" Delilah asked.

"It could be a trap. A way to swindle you out of hearth and our family home." Priscilla paused for dramatic effect, smoothing the imaginary wrinkles out of her dress before she continued her rant. "My future home is at stake, and we can't have that. Men like him are like that, preying on the bewilderment of spinsters."

Tamar raised her head, her eyes flashing anger and fury. She leveled her gaze at her sister. Priscilla took a few steps away from her, knowing that look which she gave a few times in her life meant she was past her poking and prodding point. "You don't know him."

"Neither do you," countered Priscilla as she exited the building.

"He wouldn't hurt me," Tamar said to the closed door and to Delilah. More so the words were a comfort to her. Tamar rubbed her hands over the front of her dress, pressing her palms against her stomach. A place that would never have a baby inside of it. "He wouldn't do that. He'll be back. I know it."

CHAPTER FIFTEEN

Tamar was at her desk, editing the last bit of copy for the latest edition when Delilah rushed into the office with tears streaming down her face. Before she could ask what was wrong, Delilah spoke shakily. "He is dead."

Tamar stopped, her blood chilling at the words. "Who is dead?"

Delilah cleared her throat and read from the telegram in her trembling hands. "The Deadwood Dick gang held up a train on the outskirts of Denver. Four dead. Killed in a shootout." She passed the telegram over to Tamar. "We have to write the story, even if it is weeks old. This is huge news."

Another man she loved was dead. Gone too soon.

Tamar twisted the ring on her finger. The one he'd slipped on her finger as he promised to love her and return to her.

And then everything went black.

. . .

At the same time Tamar and the *Kansas City Advocate* staff of two learned of Deadwood Dick's death, a man limped across a wide, unpaved street. He was careful to avoid the bustle of traffic, which meant doing his errands earlier in the day. Catching a look of himself in the window, he almost didn't recognize himself. The bushy beard and haphazard hair of the lawless man … gone. The dust and grime of days on the trail had been carried away. As soon as he crossed the border back into his territorial home, he headed for the nearest river and jumped in to cleanse himself in the purification ritual his ancestors did after battle.

That had been two weeks ago. Three weeks, maybe? The time was mushing together. The days didn't make sense. For weeks he had been in a drug-induced haze, recovering from his injuries.

He barely scanned the headlines while he recovered in that Omaha hospital. Bart buried the story about the shootout until Amos could escape safely back to Oklahoma. The gang was busted. The heist and all future heists were foiled. Several men met their god or were going to meet their maker during long sentences or in the hangman's gallows. He wasn't needed for the trials of those men or the alderman who masterminded the heists based on his knowledge of the rail schedules. Deadwood Dick was done and buried, through with that part of his life.

And he was free. Years of on-and-off undercover work were finished. His scars on his body and in his heart were the only things left over from that time.

Free to do what? He had everything he wanted here: his land, his family, and his heritage. All except the woman he loved and left. The woman who thought he was dead.

His fingers tightened around the cane, a now necessary device after being shot in the gut. He thought the feelings would have died gradually over time.

Foolish man. They only grew deeper. How could she trust him if he hadn't told her?

He needed to know. He needed to tell her. He owed her that modicum of truth.

Instead of going into the bank, he zigzagged across the street to the telegraph office.

The clerk collected the notes and his eyes bugged at the amount of money passed to him. "Sir, this is more than enough for a hundred telegrams."

"Make sure they get there at the times I want, son."

"Yes, sir. Is there anything else I can do for you?"

Amos stopped, pausing to let the cane absorb the pain and the weight of his body. "You're married, aren't you?" He couldn't remember the young man's name but he remembered his face—pale and doughy like a dinner roll with jolly green eyes under bushy eyebrows.

"Edwin. It's Edwin Marshall, and I'm about to be if your niece Iris agrees."

"Iris," Amos said, stroking his chin. She was the oldest of his nieces. He missed most of her childhood because he was running around for and from the law. "The teacher, correct?"

"Yes, sir."

"What do you want to do with the rest of your life? Be a teller?"

"No, I would like to own the mercantile in town."

Amos smiled. A businessman in the family. He liked the sound of that. "You need capital for that. Let's sit down and talk about a loan to make that a reality so you can provide for my niece and your eventual family."

"Oh thank you!" the young man blubbered. "This is so generous, and so— Oh my goodness, this is wonderful."

Amos raised his hand. "This will require some work. I have high expectations."

"Loving your niece is worth the work and expectations," Edwin blurted out.

Amos nodded. Love was worth the work and risk. It was good that the young man realized this early instead of getting the lesson too late. The way he had with Tamar. He shook the thought of her from his head. He had business to attend to and getting caught up thinking about her wasn't going to do him any good. "Come over later this week and we can discuss some favorable circumstances for your future," he said, rapping three times on the wood counter. At least some time this week he wouldn't be caught up in his own daydreams about the one he left behind. His business meeting gave him something to look forward to.

CHAPTER SIXTEEN

A week after the fainting spell, Tamar attempted to go back to work, but she couldn't summon the motivation to work. Lethargy consumed her body, and every morning her stomach rumbled until she gagged into the nearest bowl.

Something was wrong.

Her body was changing, and she hadn't bled at her appointed time. Her grandmother taught all the girls to watch the moon to know when their cycles would come. After four new moons, she was certain.

Priscilla and Delilah had been correct.

For once in her life, she was willing to admit that she was wrong.

Priscilla and Delilah sat on the edge of the bed and stared at their sister. "You fainted. You missed your courses." Tamar added all these things up in her head. She was with a baby.

Priscilla grabbed her hand. "We can make this go away," she said, her voice barely above a hoarse whisper. "There are women who can help us … "

"Us?" Tamar asked, propping herself up in the bed.

"You. Help you if you wanted to—"

"You don't have much time if you wanted to dispose of the—" Delilah searched for the words. "If you wanted to not be with the baby."

"I can't make a decision like that without—" Tamar's voice cracked as the tears filled her eyes. "Without seeing him one last time."

Delilah and Priscilla spoke in unison, their words jumbled. "Do we know him? Is he in town? I'll kill him."

"He's dead."

"Dead?"

Priscilla gasped. "You're carrying the baby of a man named Deadwood Dick? Sister, I know you are sophisticated with all your women's suffrage but a baby outside of the boundaries of marriage and with a man with that nickname. Deadwood Dick, seriously?"

Delilah beamed as she squealed with delight. "A baby with an outlaw. How romantic!"

Priscilla shot a steely and withering glare at her youngest sister. "Freeman women don't have children outside of holy matrimony and the marital bed. We must do something about this."

Tamar sighed. Her sisters, bless their hearts, wanted the best for her, and she wanted them off her bed and away from her. "I am going to do something."

"Good," Priscilla said, patting the quilt stretched across the bed. "I will call on Miss Eliza and ask her discreetly for the herbs to make the vile concoction—"

A scowl crept across Tamar's face. "Do nothing of that sort."

"You cannot be serious, Tamar. This baby isn't—"

"This baby is mine, and this baby is his." Tamar crossed her arms over her midsection. "I didn't plan on the baby or falling in love with him."

Delilah sighed again. Tamar was going to have to speak with her about her overly romantic sighing before she left for Howard in the coming year. She had to toughen up the girl. "I think it's beautiful. Unconquerable love across life and death. Romeo and Juliet have nothing on this."

"She isn't wed. How are we going to explain this? What will this do to Charles?" Priscilla whined.

Tamar didn't need the reminder about the constant nagging male presence in her life. "Charles is your concern, not mine. And I can make do. I will find a way or make one."

"You have my support," Delilah volunteered. "I will work as hard as I can to make this work."

Priscilla reluctantly clasped her sister's hand. "I am here for you, but Charles … I will work on him."

"What can we do?"

"I need to know where he is." Tamar's words stained the air, and the sisters looked away, wishing the words would die. "I need to know," she said again, clutching her sisters' hands.

Delilah broke the silence. "He's dead. Burial place unknown. They didn't say much about him."

"I know where he would be buried." If his family got the body, if he had family, he would be with them in his beloved homeland.

"You loved him. More than you loved any other man."

Tamar nodded, unable to form words and fiddling with the ring on her hand. "He loved me briefly, and I thank him for that. I have to visit him one last time. Delilah, you mentioned that you knew where?" she asked, wiping the tears from her eyes.

Delilah bounced off the bed and raced out of the room, returning with a clutter of telegrams in her hands. "It's in this pile. All of these have come for you]." She glanced at the notes and made a face. "Odd. Most are all from the same place."

Tamar sifted through the *Advocate* telegrams and letters that she neglected, separating them into piles. One stack she passed to Delilah for stories and editorials, who jotted down her commentary.

Priscilla thumbed through the last series on the bed, her face scrunched up in curiosity. "These don't make sense. There are just Bible verses," she said, thrusting the bunch of paper to her sister before launching off the bed. "I am headed out. I will be back later. And if you change your mind about—"

"I won't," Tamar answered, coolness easing through her voice.

Tamar scanned the messages. Her heart dropped to her feet. It had to be a coincidence. Her eyes glided over the page that was missing sentences, nouns, and verbs. All that were on these telegrams were scriptures directing her to certain places in the Bible.

The first one she knew intimately and from memory. Song of Songs. "Set me as a seal upon thine heart, as a seal upon thine arm: for love *is* strong as death; jealousy *is* cruel as the grave." Amos had whispered those words to her before he left as she lay in his arms. Tears filled her eyes, but she brushed them away. Lovers speak those words to each other, so who would send such a thing to her?

The next set referenced love and passion proverbs. The sender included her favorite: "Many waters cannot quench love." She could finish the rest of the verse by rote: " … rivers cannot wash it away. If one were to give all the wealth of his house for love, it would be utterly scorned." The final telegram had one sole word: Lazarus. Tamar pressed the bundles of papers against her chest, full of hope that what she wanted was coming true. "What chapter of the Bible is the story of Lazarus?"

"Gospel of John. Chapter eleven."

Tamar snatched the book from her sister's hands and ran a finger over the page, searching for the verse. As she stumbled over it, she read the verse aloud, "And he that was dead came forth, bound hand and foot with grave clothes: and his face was bound about with a napkin. Jesus saith unto them, Loose him, and let him go."

Maybe Amos had risen from the dead.

She threw off the covers and hopped out of the bed. She wobbled, woozy from the sleep, despair, and stress she experienced, grabbing the bedpost for support. "What's the train schedule?"

"Trains? Tamar, you just—"

"Train schedule to Oklahoma. I need that," Tamar said, still clutching the post as her world settled around her.

Delilah nodded. "I'll get that for you. Let me head to the station," she said, scooting out of the room.

Tamar called after her youngest sister. When Delilah popped back into the room, Tamar moved to the door and hugged her sister. "I entrust you to take care of everything for me while I am gone."

"Take care of what?"

"The paper. The house." Tamar smiled. "I have to see about a man who came back to life."

CHAPTER SEVENTEEN

Amos walked to the station platform's end and watched the train approach. He and the town's mayor had fought like hellcats to get the railroad to stop in this town. Without a station, this outpost would be a memory in twenty or thirty years. After all that the founding fathers and mothers of the town fought for he wouldn't see this town reduced to dust and ghosts. A thriving college was moving into town, and with statehood fast coming, they would be a beacon.

The passengers poured off the train. Some greeted him by name. Others were too terrified to speak with the man who once wore the tin star. He wasn't there for them. He was looking for one woman in the crowd of many, watching the passengers shuffle off the train. Another arrival, no sign of Tamar. He peered at the pocket watch in his hand. Everyone should be off the train by now.

He had given her a month after the last telegram.

Fool. He always met the train, and she never appeared. This would be his last time coming here and waiting and hoping like a besotted fool for his treasure to arrive. He couldn't or shouldn't expect someone to drop everything to seek him out.

She may not have even received the letter or the telegrams.

From his contacts, mostly Bart, he knew that Tamar had stepped down from her role as editor.

He hoped she didn't hate him.

He hoped she would come.

Both were proving to be false.

He would learn how to forget her. Even as the ludicrous thought popped into his mind, Amos shook his head. A man never forgot a woman like Tamar. He would never have that same intensity with another woman. He knew it. He could make do with that. At least he had those special moments with her.

He pulled out his praline and stuck one in his mouth. He closed his eyes, letting the sweetness dissolve on his tongue. Whenever he had these, he thought of her and the sweet taste of her after she had one of these.

"May I share that with you?"

He was daydreaming her voice. Amos was reluctant to open his eyes, relishing in this moment of hearing her one last time. A bare, feminine hand clutched his and tugged. "Amos, you can share with me."

She was here. His eyes flew open and took in the sight of her inches away from him. A swell of satisfaction and peace engulfed him.

Tamar spoke first. "I wasn't sure if I was right to come here. I didn't know what to expect."

"A dead man?" he asked after exhaling a long sigh of contentment.

Her slight smile broadened. "Or a man who played tricks on me."

He shook his head, still shocked at the sight before him. "Never, Tamar. I don't do tricks."

"You did lie."

"I was working for the Pinkertons. No one knew." He frowned. "I wanted to tell you."

"I'm glad you are alive." She barely had the words out when he pulled her into him.

"I've missed you, Tamar Ruth," he whispered before pecking her mouth.

"Don't tell me," she said, wrapping her arms around his neck. "Show me." She pressed her lips against his. He responded, crushing her into him. Her breasts pillowed against his chest.

They were closer than some would think appropriate in public. He didn't care. All he wanted was her and for her to know that his desire had not waned.

She sighed, and he took advantage of her slightly parted lips, tasting her tongue.

"Don't leave me again, Amos."

"Darlin', I will try my best. I didn't want to leave you that morning, but I had to. I will spend my life making that up to you if you want."

"Is that a proposal?"

"I can't get down on one knee, but I love you, Tamar. Forever and a day. My words will never match up to the feelings I have for you, but I promise to protect you fiercely, love you fiercely. You are my home where I feel safe and loved."

"I want to be your wife, your everything." She placed his hand on her stomach. "The mother to your children."

Amos's hand lingered on her midsection. The slow dawn of realization creased his face. Before he spoke, she nodded.

"This will make for a great story." He cradled her face, drinking her in. "The man who rose from the dead."

"Rumored and presumed dead."

"What about the *Advocate* and your home?"

"They will survive without me. Delilah is going to Howard soon, and she never wanted to have a newspaper. Priscilla might keep it, but—" Tamar drifted off as she stared into the distance. "I don't care. I'm here with you."

"I will buy you a paper," Amos countered. "Four papers and a good press here in Oklahoma."

"Don't make promises you can't keep, Amos."

"For you, my love, there are not any promises I won't keep," he muttered against her lips before sealing the promise with a kiss.

She broke away, directing her dazzling smile at the man in front of her. "I could have this with you for forever."

Amos nodded, pressing his fingers against his lips. He had everything. His love. His land. His name and his rightful self. Soon there would be a wedding and a baby. "Tamar, I want this for a couple of forevers, for centuries to come."

Together, they walked away from the train station and into town, in search of a good meal, glowing in love.

A SNEAK PEEK FROM CRIMSON ROMANCE

Fool for You
Rina Gray

If Wile E. Coyote ever successfully trapped the Road Runner, he'd have the same just-won-the-lotto grin as Melanie Foster.

She texted her best friend, Damien, the thumbs-up, prayer hands, and dancing hippo emojis—he'd get that she had good news to share. He always got her. Striding up to the receptionist counter at her brand-spanking-new job, she glanced at the woman's nameplate. *Meena.* No last name. Just Meena.

"Meena, you are now looking at the new associate editor for SportsFanatic.com. I got the job!" Melanie sang and moonwalked backward in her stilettos. Well, she tried and tripped. Not smart considering she wasn't much of a high-heel enthusiast. Luckily, she managed to grab the counter for balance before the hardwood floor became the most action she'd had in eighteen months.

"Good for you." The receptionist rolled her brown, Betty Boop eyes and resumed her clicking and clacking on the keyboard.

Melanie gave her a strained smile. *Seriously?* This chick didn't get how awesome this was. Not only had Melanie scored the associate editor position at SportsFanatic.com, but she was also the first African-American female editor for the online magazine. And, to make her dream job even more amazing—like triple-fudge-brownie-with-hazelnuts-and-caramel amazing—she would be the exclusive writer for the Yankees. The freakin' New. York. Yankees.

The receptionist leaned away from the desk and folded her slender arms. "You haven't started the job yet so … bye?"

"Let's do lunch when I start. My treat. See you soon!" Melanie pivoted toward the elevator, all smiles on the outside but mentally flipping the finger with both hands on the inside. Meena would not kill her vibe.

Pressing the down button, Melanie slid her wire-framed glasses back on her nose, tapped her toes, and waited. Under her breath, she hummed a celebratory got-the-job song. This needed to be celebrated. Nearly all her goals had been achieved. Bomb.com job: Check. Next item: Convince her best friend to be the father of her two-point-five kids and live in a brownstone in Chelsea. *Is there such a thing as half a check?* A ding from the arriving elevator answered her.

But she wasn't worried. If she could beat out eighty-seven candidates for her dream job, she could win the heart of her dream man. The elevator doors slid shut, and she let loose.

"I just got the jooob. I just got the joooob! Happy job dance, happy job dance!" She diva-fied her dancing with a hip swirl that would make the founders of Zumba proud.

The elevator dinged, groaned, and stopped on the ground floor. She walked out of the ancient elevator and, with each step, closer to her best friend.

Damien. Damien. Damien. Just thinking of his Georgia-pecan eyes and quiet storm voice made her palms slick and her heart beat strong and funky like an old Motown bass line.

Writing kick-ass articles about kick-ass athletes? That she could do. The tall task of convincing her BFF to fall in love with her and do the tangled tango? That loomed over her like the Empire State Building.

A needle of fear popped her optimistic bubble. Sifting through the deep grooves of her memories, she desperately sought where she could've gotten the wrong impression. Had she imagined their connection—the hungry stares, the almost kisses, the soul-tingling touches?

Their soul-mate bond was the reason why she couldn't move on. So she'd bided her time, kept it casual with other men, until she couldn't bear the thought of another woman in his arms.

There was a hole at the bottom of her heart, and no other man's kiss, or touch, or words could fill it. It was only and always Damien. The boy who'd defended her from neighborhood bullies, taught her how to field a ground ball, and took her to senior prom when her date had bailed at the last minute.

The boy who eventually grew into a man who cooked her favorite meals when she came into town, gave her autographed memorabilia from her favorite athletes, and flew her up to New York when her favorite boy bands, one of her guilty pleasures, were in concert.

His deep voice whispered in her head. "Babe, you don't know what you're asking. You're upset about breaking up with your boyfriend, and you want me because I'm familiar."

Pausing before the door of the building, she opened her large purse and rubbed her thumbs over the familiar frayed seams of the baseball cap Damien had placed onto her head before she hit her first home run. Her lucky hat instantly unraveled the double fisherman knots of doubt that had settled in the bottom of her stomach.

Damien loves me. He's just scared.

Pulling out her phone, she opened the notes app to review the list she'd created for Operation: I'm Gonna Make You Love Me. She tapped the screen to mark off the first step: get the job in New York. Now, she needed to find a place near his condo and figure out a way to spend time with him.

Easy. She grinned down at her phone. There was always a game on television, and if their favorite team wasn't playing, there were action flicks or the obscure kung fu movies they'd both collected over the sixteen years they'd known each other. And if she was lucky, she could convince him to watch an occasional rom-com. Her eyes froze at the next item on her list: Vanessa. *Not so easy.*

Damien was currently dating his boss's daughter. But from the few conversations Melanie had had with her best friend about the woman, it didn't seem serious.

You've got this. Feeling confident about her next steps, she shoved her phone into her purse and smiled.

Melanie pushed open the front door and walked into a cacophony of car horns, skipping over a slush puddle and sidestepping a Chinese deliveryman. Everyone looked rushed and hurried like contestants on *The Amazing Race.* And she absolutely loved it. She'd miss her friends in Atlanta, but New York would be her new home. Her pulse skyrocketed at the thought of finally living within minutes of her best friend. Taking a cue from her new city, she picked up the pace to share her good news with Damien. Operation: I'm Gonna Make You Love Me was now in action.

• • •

Damien Richards, public relations director extraordinaire, drummed his fingers on his large oak desk. He stared at a video of his client, a basketball center recently nominated for defensive player of the year. White fur jacket, fedora hat with a zebra-print band, and diamond-encrusted cane. Stumbling around his Bentley. Drunk.

Damien grabbed his phone and pressed the voice-to-text button. "Research methods to break Aaron's cane, then schedule meeting with idiot client. Avoid beating aforementioned idiot with remaining pieces as this is generally frowned upon by HR."

Reaching into his desk, he pulled out his stash of gummy bears and scooped a handful into his mouth. *Nice.* An extra bag was tucked in the drawer corner. God bless his assistant, Charlotte, who anticipated his sugar cravings when clients did TMZ-worthy screw-ups.

"Damien," Charlotte buzzed from the intercom. "Ms. Leslie Taylor on line one for you."

"All right." Leslie was the founder and executive director of Refurbished Dreams, the organization that had steered him away from a troubled path when he was younger and where he currently volunteered his time as a mentor. "And thanks for the gummies. I needed the extra bag."

Her light and airy laugh softened his aggravation with Aaron. "No problem, boss."

Damien clicked off the line and pressed the blinking red button. "Hey, Les. Thought I already told you I'd swing by to volunteer today?"

"Damien I … I have some bad news."

Leslie's voice, soft and foreboding, revved his heartbeat.

"What happened?"

"Th-they … The bank. They're closing us down. Oh, God. After fifteen years, hundreds of kids, thousands of hours, all the good Refurbished Dreams has done, and all the kids we've saved … What are my kids gonna do now?"

Leslie's "kids" were high school to college aged, but she loved them as if they were her own.

Damien massaged the bass-drum throb at his temple. Cursing softly, he tried to find the right words for the woman who had saved his life. "You know how much I owe you. Hell, if it wasn't for you and Refurbished Dreams, I'd be wearing orange jumpsuits instead of business suits." His voice lowered, infusing the conversation with cool and calm. "I'll do anything within my power to help."

"That's why I called you." Leslie's high-pitched voice teetered on the edge of desperation. "The bank is foreclosing the loan for the mortgage."

He'd never heard her so panicked, so anxious, so alarmed. Her infamous optimism had been wrung dry.

"How much time do we have, and how much do we owe?" He tried to quash his accusatory tone. Leslie hadn't been the best at keeping the nonprofit in the black.

"We have until the first of April to pay. Two hundred and fifty thousand."

A month? That was no time at all to convince someone to cut a check. And a quarter of a million dollars would only temporarily plug the ever-growing hole at the bottom of the barrel.

He pinched the bridge of his nose. "We'll set up a meeting and ask for more time. I already applied for the grant at my agency." It was only for fifty thousand, so it wouldn't cover everything, but it would help. "Did you have any luck with grants on your end?"

"No. The company awarded the money to a nonprofit that serves terminally ill children and an organization that supports literacy."

He couldn't see Leslie but could guess from the steady squeak that she was rocking back and forth in her rickety leather office chair. And, if he were a gambling man, he'd place a bet that right about now she was chewing on a pen.

"Let's face it, those companies don't see us as saving lives. If it weren't for us, our kids would be back on the streets or worse." Her tone turned as bitter as a January morning in New York.

Damien nodded, thinking back on his checkered past. Idle hands were the devil's playground, and when a poor kid with real talent dreams of becoming a sports star were no longer a reality due to an injury, he was a sitting duck for getting pulled into the streets.

If the injury could be managed, Refurbished Dreams helped the young athletes rehab and get back on track. If the injury was too extensive, like Damien's had been, they'd help find another dream in sports through mentorship.

Leslie had yanked him from his depression, pulled him away from the lure of selling drugs, and placed him with a mentor, now his boss, in sports marketing. Leslie had saved him, and he'd become a champion for their cause. But he wasn't always victorious, and he'd recently lost a mentee to a gang war.

"We can't fail them … like Roger." Heavy and heartsick, Damien's voice became weighed down by 180 pounds of guilt for a life he hadn't been able to save. A snake unfurled in the pit of his stomach then slithered and rattled in his chest when he thought of his mentee. Talented. Funny. So full of life. Until he wasn't.

"What should we do?" Leslie asked.

"I'll check with my boss to see if he can speed up my grant proposal. Why don't you look up past donors and sponsors? Then we'll hit the phones, shake some hands, and send out a few email blasts."

"That might just work." A spark of hope ignited Leslie's tone.

"All right, Les. I gotta go make some calls. Talk to you soon."

"Okay, bye. And Damien? Thanks. I'm sorry I lost it for a few, but I'm back now. I'm good."

Damien took off the phone headset, clicked into his boss's online calendar, and found an opening in thirty minutes. He sent a meeting request to Leonard James's secretary. Leonard wasn't only his boss—he'd been Damien's own mentor at Refurbished Dreams when Damien was in college. Leslie had saved him and given him options, but Leonard had inspired him, groomed him, taken him to client meetings that most men his age wouldn't attend—and not until they had a senior in front of their title. The man had seen something in Damien. Maybe the son he never had? Damien's father, dead for several years now, had never taken the time to nurture their relationship. Melvin Richards had only had time for work and broken promises.

Because Refurbished Dreams meant something to Leonard too, Damien was hopeful he'd help them out with the grant money.

Leaning back in his chair, he swiveled to face his office door. The white bookcase holding a dozen trophies and awards caught his attention, but the homing beacon was the game ball given to him at the College World Series. He walked over to grab the prize and rolled it around his fingers.

Memories rushed in—his full athletic scholarship, being drafted by the Dodgers, the injury that killed his shoulder. The injury that killed his dreams.

Tossing the ball up, he quickly caught it. A soft ding sounded from the computer, and he dropped the ball on the floor and jammed his finger on the keyboard to view the screen.

"Yes!" Electricity zapped his heart into overdrive. Leonard had accepted the impromptu meeting. Now, Damien just needed to convince his boss and mentor to fork over the big bucks.

In the mood for more Crimson Romance?
Check out *The Herald's Heart by Rue Allyn*
at CrimsonRomance.com.

www.ingramcontent.com/pod-product-compliance
Lightning Source LLC
Chambersburg PA
CBHW010305100726

47904CB00011B/2753